He stood gazing into the room. Throughout the house was a great and pervasive silence.

Shan stepped into the room and then halted abruptly. There was something white and shimmering on his bureau.

He went slowly to it and saw that it was an envelope.

Outside the street light went on, and its ray pierced through the darkness and fell on the white envelope. Now he saw that his name was written on it.

Shan picked up the envelope, opened it, and took out a card. He held it up to the light and slowly read what was written on it.

It said: Happy Birthday, Murderer.

The handwriting was his own.

JAY BENNETT has won the Edgar Award twice for his two mysteries from Delacorte Press: *The Long Black Coat* and *The Dangling Witness.* His previous mystery, *Say Hello to the Hit Man,* was called "fast-paced [and] involving" by *Booklist.* All three books are available in Laurel-Leaf editions. Mr. Bennett lives in New York City.

THE LAUREL-LEAF LIBRARY brings together under a single imprint outstanding works of fiction and nonfiction particularly suitable for young adult readers, both in and out of the classroom. The series is under the editorship of Charles F. Reasoner, Professor of Elementary Education, New York University.

The Birthday Murderer

A MYSTERY
BY

Jay Bennett

For
Steve, Jan, and Ceyenna Renoir
Tombé, Joshua, and Old Babuf

The
Birthday
Murderer

I

It started with the birthday party. He had not wanted it, but his mother had insisted.

"It's your seventeenth birthday, Shan."

"I know. But . . ."

"You'll be going away soon. I'll be alone. I feel like filling the house with people having fun."

"But I'll be home every other weekend, Mother."

"I'll still feel lonely."

He wanted to say, You'll have Paul Lambert, so you won't be alone. You see him so much. He wanted to say it, but he felt that his jealousy would creep into his voice, and he didn't want that to happen.

She touched his hand gently. "Let's give a party."

He was silent.

1

"All right?"

He shifted away from her a bit and looked out the window at the gray September day. No one was on the sidewalk below. The trees were tall and motionless. He felt the emptiness of the street surge up and into him.

She spoke the same words, this time adding his name, but he didn't hear her. Somehow he felt withdrawn from her. Lately he had been feeling that way—withdrawn not only from her, but from all things. He didn't know why.

"I don't care much for birthday parties," he said.

"You used to."

"I was a kid then."

"Shan, I thought you enjoyed your last one." Her voice was gentle, and her eyes were smiling.

"Maybe it was just an act," he said. Yet he knew that she was right. He had enjoyed his last party.

"An act?"

"All I know is that I don't care for birthday parties anymore," he said in a low voice, "don't care to have them or to go to them."

Her smile was gone. "Why?"

He felt her dark eyes searching him. "I just don't," he said. Again he didn't know why, but lately that was how he felt.

"You're going to college," she said, trying another tack. "Doesn't that merit a party?"

He shook his head. "I'd just rather not have it."

Her voice had a pleading tone to it. "For me, Shan. I'd get such pleasure out of giving it. And I know you'll enjoy it."

He was silent. Outside the leaves of the trees wavered for an instant. They were beginning to lose their green, turning red and brown. It's just beginning, he thought. But it will happen fast. Autumn is coming fast, and then it will be winter. Cold, dead winter.

"Well?"

He kept his eyes fixed on the leaves, and all of a sudden he felt that they were blazing with fiery sunlight, in a cluster of golden flames. But there was no sunlight. The sky was gray and flat. Then the image vanished, as swiftly as it had come. The fire was gone, and he saw the leaves as they were, motionless against the leaden sky. It had all happened so quickly.

"Shannon?"

He turned to his mother and sighed. He saw her eyes on him, so he shrugged his shoulders, smiled wearily, and said, "Okay. Go ahead with it."

Her face seemed to light up in a little glow of triumph. "Thanks," she said.

"But keep it small." He smiled.

"I will."

That's how it all started—slow and subtle and quiet— the terror he felt.

She left him alone in his room, looking out the window, thinking, his shadow angled on the wall.

Seventeen, he thought. I'll soon be seventeen. Lately he had found himself thinking about that. Lately he felt that there was something significant in the number. Seventeenth birthday. Now, a party. He felt that some- where within him he knew why it was significant and terrifying. Now, as he stood there, he consciously tried to penetrate to the secret. But he couldn't. There was only a vague, amorphous feeling. He shook his head, close to despair.

"My seventeenth birthday," he said aloud. His own voice startled him.

After a while he turned and went slowly to the opposite window. He stood gazing down into a garden, a small, tangled garden that ended with an iron fence. Beyond the rusting black fence was a narrow, grassy lane and then the first trees and meadows of Prospect Park.

The house itself was an old, narrow brownstone with three floors. His father had bought it twelve years ago, when it was a good buy. Then, after his sudden death, Shan's mother had converted the first floor into a small apartment, which she rented out. But after a bad experience with a tenant, and not really needing the money, she stopped renting the apartment and left it vacant. She and Shan continued to live on the other two floors.

Calvin Rourke, father. Margaret Rourke, mother. Shannon Rourke, son. Only son. You're the last of an ancient and sturdy tree, his father had said to him one night. They were out in the garden. His voice was low and melodious. His big hand rested gently and lovingly on Shan's knee. Make sure you live and have children, he had said. And then his father had died.

Shan was tall, lean, and handsome, with reddish-blond hair and fair skin. He stood looking down into the garden, letting the names and memories pass through his consciousness.

You're the last, Shan. Be sure you live. The last.

As the words echoed and faded, his dark blue eyes

became somber. Be sure you live, his father had said, and there had been a strange expression on his pale face.

Was it fear? Shan thought. He used to look at me. Just look at me. What did he know that he never told me?

He didn't fear for himself. No, I'm sure of that. It was for me. But why? Why?

"Be sure you live," Shan whispered.

He turned, almost expecting to see his father standing by his side. Then Shan breathed in deeply and turned back to the window.

The house was the last one on a block of old houses. At night, when the street lights went on, this end of the block had the quietness and emptiness of a stage set just after the curtain goes up, with no one yet on stage. It was particularly true in late fall and winter, when people stayed inside their homes.

Many times Shan had looked down from his room on the third floor, down into the well of lamplight, and felt the eerie sense of a play about to begin. If a figure appeared on the lit sidewalk, he would watch it move, follow every step, till it finally disappeared into the night. And Shan would wonder about the figure and try to create a history and a drama for it. Even a destiny.

At times he would go to the other window, his eyes seeking out the garden, searching its shadows and glints of lights.

Just before evening set in, when he was younger, about eight or nine, he would go to the corridor and then down the staircase and out the door and along the path that led into the garden. He would do it all silently and stealthily, his nerves tingling until he stepped out into the pure stillness of the garden. He would pause, letting it envelop him. His clear features would be taut and alert. The fading light of the day would tint his figure. He would stand motionless.

Then he would breathe in deeply and let his imagination have full sway. He would think himself set down in a vast, impenetrable jungle. All about him were fierce and death-dealing animals. And he, Shannon Rourke, was the hunter, lone and fearless, ready to track down his savage enemies and kill them ruthlessly. Yes, kill them.

Shan would imagine himself stepping forward and entering the hostile jungle. The relentless hunt would begin, it always ended with a muted cry of triumph.

Sometimes he would reverse the roles. Shan would become the hunted: lone, weaponless, and fearful, dreading each approaching footfall. Ready to scream a silent scream of terror should the panther with the glowing eyes suddenly crash through the thicket and leap for his throat.

And so he would play until darkness came, and with it the voice of his mother, searching for him in one of the rooms above.

There was a stone bench in the garden, just under the branches of a broad plane tree. Sometimes—this happened after his father's death—he would imagine the man sitting there, a sharply outlined figure, quietly watching Shan play. His eyes would be smiling, and yet quietly, ever so quietly, he would appraise his son. Just as he often did when he was alive.

After a while his father would lean forward and take out a cigar and light it, his movements deliberate, his eyes fixed steadily on the boy. The sudden flaming of the match would make Shan go cold with fear and guilt. He would stand rigid, his face white, his eyes large and staring, until finally the flame was blotted out by the oncoming darkness.

Shan would sigh softly and then begin to play again. But every time he looked back to the bench—and he couldn't stop himself from doing that—he would see the end of the cigar glowing like an eye in the darkness. A large, accusing, vengeful eye that seemed to approach and finally to burn into him with such intensity that he would want to shout to his father, Stamp out the eye. Stamp it out. Please. Please.

"Please." With the whispered word, he would realize that he was imagining it all. His father was not sitting there on the bench. There was no glowing eye. There was nobody on the bench.

His father was dead.

Now, as Shan stood looking down at the bench, dull white in the gray light of the September day, he felt that somehow his father knew the secret. About the significance of the seventeenth birthday.

Seventeenth.

"I don't remember," Shan whispered. But deep within him he knew that he did remember. There had been a seventeenth birthday for someone else. Shan was there as a child. But he had blotted out the memory, just as the darkness had blotted out the flame.

Because something terrible and searing had happened at the party. Someone had lit a match . . . and then there was a flame . . . and then a scream . . . an agonizing scream . . .

7

"I don't remember," Shan whispered and turned away from the window.

Outside a breeze came up, and the leaves of the trees wavered and shook. One leaf fell from its branch as if a knife had cut it off in a savage slash. The leaf fluttered to the ground and then lay there, motionless and dead.

II

He called Donna Carson. She was the first person he invited to the party.

"You're the first one, Donna."

"I know, Shan. But I can't come."

"Why?"

"It's one of those things. Got to go to Scranton for a family party. I just can't get out of it."

"Sure you can."

"No chance."

"Just say you don't want to go. You can sleep over here till they come back. You've slept here before. You know how welcome you are in this house."

"It's a wedding, Shan."

"Oh." He knew there was no getting out of that.

"Happy birthday, Shan," he heard her say. "Happy birthday, just the same."

"Thanks, Donna," he said softly into the phone.

"I'm sorry."

"I know you are. With me it's . . ." His voice trailed off, and they didn't speak for a moment.

"A wedding," she said. "People are still getting married. What do you think of that, Shan?" She laughed.

He sat there, listening to her laughter and feeling a warm glow. Her voice was gentle and rippling. He imagined her face before him, open and appealing.

"I'll see you when I come back," she said. "Okay?"

"Sure thing, Donna."

"So long, Shan."

"So long."

But she didn't hang up. "My father wants me to drive most of the way once we get out of the city. He says he drives enough all week on the job."

"He sure does. He's got a long run, Donna."

"I know, but it's not that at all. He gets a kick out of me driving. It makes him proud because he taught me."

There was something else she wanted to talk about. Knowing her, he waited, while he continued the conversation.

"Could be that," he said. "But just the same, he—" Shan stopped, because he could see her shaking her head, her long dark hair swinging.

"But it isn't. I know bus drivers that love to drive on weekends. Lots of my father's friends do."

"That's because their wives make them do it, Donna," he said.

"What?"

"That's right." He could see her putting her chin out, her black eyes snapping.

"Stop blaming the wives. You can do better than that."

"I'm just kidding, trying to get a rise out of you."

"You can still do better."

"Okay." He smiled. "Okay." He knew she was now smiling, too.

"These guys just can't get away from the wheel. That's what it is, Shan. They see a driving wheel and they respond to it."

"You mean a steering wheel."

"So I mean a steering wheel. They want to put their hands around it. In a way, they're nuts."

"Aren't we all?"

"No. Just you and me."

He laughed.

"I'll miss you, Shan," she said.

He nodded as if she could see him and said, "It'll be the same with me."

There was a pause, and then he heard "Have a good party."

Still she didn't hang up. Now he waited; soon she would tell him what was really concerning her. He wondered what it was.

"Oh, Shan."

"Yes."

Her voice was hesitant. "There's something I want to talk to you about."

"Go ahead."

"I don't know." She seemed to be fumbling. It wasn't like her. "I . . . maybe it can wait till we can see each other."

"What is it?"

"When I get back, Shan."

But he pressed on. "I wish you'd tell me."

"Well, it's . . . something about you lately."

He felt a chill go through him.

"I don't know how to put my finger on it. It's a feeling, Shan. That's all it is. A feeling."

He waited.

"A feeling that something's wrong with you. Is there?"

"What do you mean?"

"You seem terribly worried about something."

"I don't know what you're talking about," he said. His voice was sharp.

"Is it Lambert?"

"What?"

"Paul Lambert."

"Why him?"

"Every time he's around I see you kind of tighten up."

"I'm not aware of that," he said, almost curtly.

"There's almost a scared look about you."

"Scared?" Now he was getting angry at her.

"Are you afraid that he'll marry your mother, and you don't want that?"

"Marry her?"

He felt a hot flush of fear go through him, and then it was gone.

"Why not? She likes him. He seems to like her."

He was silent. What she was saying was true.

"Or is it something about the man that . . . that reminds you of something."

"Reminds me?" He was aware that he was picking up her key words and repeating them. It unnerved him all the more. "Reminds me of what?"

"You get that kind of look in your eyes."

"Donna, let it alone, will you?"

But she wouldn't. "I don't know. I've been thinking a lot about you, Shan, and I don't know."

"To hell with it, Donna. You're not making sense."

"Maybe I'm not. But I've known you for three years, Shan. I think I have a good idea of what makes you tick by now."

"You sure?" he said grimly.

"Something seems to have happened to you ever since Lambert started seeing your mother."

"Like what?"

"Can't put my finger on it. Told you that. It's a feeling."

"And yet you say you know what makes me tick."

"Well, I—"

"Listen," he cut in. "I like Lambert. And I don't know what you're talking about."

"I know you like him. I like him too. There's a lot to like about him. But just the same, when you—"

"Let's drop it. Okay?"

He heard a gentle sigh. "Okay, Shan."

"Have a good trip," he said, and his voice was softer.

"And you a good party."

"Sure thing."

Then he waited for the click. When it came, he put the telephone down slowly and sat in the chair for a long while, till his mother came into the room. Somehow he felt that she had been listening, standing just beyond the threshold and listening.

But he wasn't sure.

III

It was a bright and happy afternoon. The sun was out after many gray days. It shone through the windows into the house. The voices seemed to sound brighter in the sunlight. The laughter seemed merrier. The party was a success. Shan missed Donna, and he had been disturbed by what she had said, yet now he felt good. He glanced at his mother. She was sitting and talking to Paul Lambert. Shan thought of the night ahead. He was looking forward to going to the theater with them. The tickets were Lambert's birthday gift to him.

"I think you're going to like the play, Shan," Lambert had said when he handed Shan the envelope.

"From what I've heard of it I know I will, Paul."

"The seats are good, they're in the third row center."

"You always try for the best, Paul."

"I believe I do."

"And you get it."

"When I can." Lambert had laughed quietly. He had a pleasant, controlled voice. He was tall, just a bit taller than Shan. In a way, Lambert reminded him of his father. The man was in his late fifties, and his hair, thick and wavy, had begun to gray. He had a lithe and easy-moving body; he got in a game of tennis every morning. "I play all year long, Shan. Winter, indoors. Spring and the rest of the year, outdoors. No matter where I am. You might call me a monomaniac when it comes to that." His voice had shaded just a bit as he said again, "A monomaniac." His eyes seemed to penetrate into Shan. Then he laughed quietly and went on. "I must have my tennis or my day is lost." His hands were large and well formed. His face was lean, tanned, and sharply outlined. His eyes were large and gray. He was an attractive and poised man.

Now, as Shan stood looking at him, he kept thinking of how Lambert had come back into their lives. It was his mother who had used the words "come back." And Shan had looked strangely at her, for he could not remember the man.

"We used to know the Lamberts when we lived on the coast, Shan," his mother had said. "You were only five then. Do you remember?"

"We did live out on the coast," Shan said. "I do remember that. We had a small house, almost as small as a bungalow. And there was a lake, not far away."

His mother nodded. "There was," she said.

"I sometimes think of the house and the lake. The house becomes very clear to me. I can even see its gray shingles."

"We were happy there, Shan," she said in a low voice.

"Yes. And I liked going to the lake."

"Your father and I used to take you there often. We had happy times."

They both were silent. Then his mother said, "But you don't remember Paul Lambert."

Shan shook his head.

"Nothing about him?" she asked.

"Nothing," he said. But he felt that his mother was appraising him as he said the words, that she was trying to probe whether he really did remember. In a way, he felt that she didn't believe him.

This had happened a few months before, on an evening in July. Shan had been sitting in the living room, reading, when he heard the front door open, and then he saw his mother come into the room with a tall, graying man. The instant Shan saw him, a tremor went through him. He couldn't understand why. But the time Lambert spent with them turned out to be pleasant. Shan liked the man. It was after he had left that Shan and his mother began going back into the past and stirring up memories.

"I remember nothing about him," Shan said.

She seemed to sigh.

"Tell me more about him," Shan said.

"He used to teach psychology at the University of Southern California. Now he's alone and has come east. He's been offered a good job at Purchase, as chairman of the department. So he's looked me up."

"Is he going to take the job?"

"It seems so."

"And you say he's alone now?"

"Yes."

"But he had a family?"

"Yes. A wife and son."

"What happened to them?"

She looked away from him.

"What happened to them?" he asked again. Something seemed to be pressing him. He had to know.

"The wife divorced him."

"And the son?"

"The son is dead, Shan."

For a while they didn't speak.

"How did he die?"

"Why do you want to know?"

He shrugged. "Just curious, I guess," he said, as casually as he could. Now the pressing was like an ache in him. He waited for her to speak.

"He died in an accident, Shan," she said.

"How, Mother?"

Her face was pale. She was a small, delicate woman, and still quite pretty, yet it seemed to him now that she had become tense and, for an instant, old. Her fair, high color was gone from her cheeks, and her skin looked wrinkled, especially around her soft, blue eyes. Her hands trembled.

"There was a fire. And he was burned to death."

"Oh." His voice was soft, like a sigh.

"It was an accident, Shan," she said again.

A breeze had come up, and it rustled the curtains in

the room. He watched them moving, so gentle and so graceful.

For some reason he thought of flames. The flickering of flames. And back in the dim corners of his mind he heard a scream. A scream of a death agony.

"Shan?"

He turned back to her.

"You shivered," she said. Her eyes were searching him.

"It was nothing."

They stood facing each other.

"What is it, Shan? You're white."

"How old was he?"

She hesitated.

"Mother?"

"Why do you ask that?"

He found himself shrugging again. "I'm curious."

Pathetically, she seemed to be trying to end the conversation without knowing how to do it. In a way he wished she would end it, but they went on, as if both of them had been caught in a web of memory. Caught fast.

"Oh, about your age," she said, and he could barely hear her voice.

"Going on seventeen?"

"Just seventeen."

He thought about it, and then found himself asking a question that bewildered him, for he didn't know where it came from. Yet it seemed so inevitable to ask it. "Was I there when it happened?"

She stared at him.

"Was I there?"

"Yes," she said.

Suddenly he didn't want to ask any more questions.

"You were five then."

He turned to her. "Five?"

"You were very small."

"And I was there? I heard him scream?"

She didn't speak.

"I should remember," he said in a low voice. "That's old enough to remember." He seemed to forget that she was in the room with him. He stood there alone, trying to reach back into the past.

"You were a small child," she said.

He still didn't hear her.

"But I don't," he said, and shook his head in disbelief.

"No. You remember nothing," she said.

"Why is that?"

She kept looking at him and then she said, "I don't know." But he felt that she did know and for some reason would not tell him, so he asked no more questions.

Now, as Shan looked at Lambert, smiling and talking to his mother at the party, he knew why Paul Lambert reminded him of his father. Both men, at times, when you caught them off guard, had an agony deep in the back of their eyes. Only it seemed to Shan that Lambert's was the more haunting.

IV

"Now don't keep me waiting, Margaret,"
Lambert said in a gentle voice. "I know Shan
will be ready. But you. . ."

"I'll be ready, Paul."

The party was over. Lambert was to come back in an
hour and take them to the theater.

"We don't want to miss the first scene. It's quite
important."

"We won't, Paul."

"Good. I had an excellent time. Thanks for inviting
me."

"It was good having you."

He stood looking at Margaret, smiling at her, and
then he turned to Shan and shook his hand. "I was glad
to be with your friends, Shan. To be accepted."

It was a firm clasp. His eyes looked clearly at Shan. And yet, for an instant Shan thought he could see a fierce and bitter agony.

"They liked you," Shan said.

"I enjoyed them very much. I haven't been to a birthday party in a long time, Shan," he said. "A long time." The face was serene and the voice quiet and controlled. "I'll see you later."

Then the door closed after him. And it seemed to Shan that the sound of the closing of the door, a sharp and final sound, signaled the end of the party. Blotted it out. The light of the sun, the brightness of the voices, the birthday gifts, the birthday wishes . . . all was over. As if it never happened. The good feeling was gone. Another feeling that was always there seemed to rise within him.

He started up the staircase to his room. The shadows of evening came through the narrow hall windows and onto his face and figure. Only he and his mother were in the house now. And as he climbed the steps, one by one, the shadows lengthening on the wall, a strange and un-reasoning fear came over him, and he longed to call down to his mother, as he used to when he was a small child, alone in his room.

So this was it, your seventeenth-birthday party, he said to himself. And now it's over. Or is it?

"Mother," he called suddenly.

There was a silence after the sound of his voice. Then he heard the door of her room open.

"Shan?"

He stood on the landing, gripping the banister, looking down till he saw her. He was about to say to her, I just wanted to see your face again. That's all. Just that. Just to see it. But the words wouldn't come. Something within him, strange and puzzling, was blocking him off from her. Isolating him from her tenderness. And he wanted that so desperately. He always wanted it.

"Shan?"

"I . . . I wanted to . . ." His voice trailed away.

"Yes?"

I wanted to tell you I got scared.

"Should I shave?" he asked.

Something scared me. Tell me, Mother. Tell me what it is.

"Shave?"

"Do you think I need to?"

You know. I'm sure you know.

"Do I, Mother?"

She smiled at him, yet her face seemed pale. "You know best, Shan." Pale in the glimmering shadows. Her eyes dark and probing.

"Yes, I do," he said slowly.

Maybe deep inside I do, Mother. And that is why I am so scared. So chilled.

"Better hurry, Shan."

"Yes," he said.

Then he stood there till he heard her door close—a rustling sound. He moved away from the landing and slowly went up the remaining steps, thinking of the silly question he had asked her. Do I need a shave? And the way she had looked at him when he asked it.

He came to the threshold of his room and paused. He had left the shades of the windows half up, and now the darkness was flowing in, slowly, inexorably.

The street lights had not yet come on. In the heavy,

lowering sky he caught a glimpse of a sliver of moon, pale and thin.

He stood gazing into the room. Throughout the house was a great and pervasive silence. He felt a hovering, a hovering of a terror about to begin.

Shan stepped into the room and then halted abruptly, as if he had been a soldier, ordered to stop. His eyes were fixed ahead of him, staring. For there was something white and shimmering on his bureau.

He went slowly to it and saw that it was an envelope.

Outside the street light went on, and its ray pierced through the darkness and fell on the white envelope. Now he saw that his name was written on it.

Shan picked up the envelope, opened it, and took out a card. He held it up to the light and slowly read what was written on it.

It said: *Happy Birthday, Murderer.*

The handwriting was his own.

V

It was during intermission that Lambert
spoke to him. They were standing in a corner
of the crowded lobby, waiting for his mother
to rejoin them.

"You seem unusually quiet, Shan."

"Do I?"

"Yes. I've been watching you. You don't seem to be
responding to the play."

"I like it," Shan said.

"But not as much as you thought you would."

Shan shrugged. "I guess that's it."

"Any particular reason?"

"No. Just don't seem to be able to get with it."

"Ah," Lambert murmured.

"That's all it is."

Lambert smiled and shook his head. "It's not the play at all. It's something else, Shan."

"What do you mean, Paul?"

"I don't know exactly. But you're troubled."

The large gray eyes looked coolly and steadily at him. For an instant Shan felt that the man did know what was troubling him. Then he shook the thought away.

"It's really nothing, Paul," he said.

"Girl trouble? I noticed your friend Donna wasn't at the party."

"She couldn't make it," Shan said. "Had to go out of town with her family."

"Oh."

"It's not Donna," Shan said.

"Shan."

"Yes?"

"I teach psychology, and I'm your friend. Shan, I feel that something is deeply disturbing you."

Shan was silent.

"I sense a bit of fear in you, too."

"Fear?"

"Yes. What is it?"

They stood looking at each other, while the smoke and the voices spun about them. Then suddenly, out of a strange and compelling impulse that he couldn't understand, Shan took the envelope out of his jacket pocket and held it up.

"I found this on my bureau this evening," he said.

The man looked questioningly at him as he took the envelope.

"Someone had gone into my room and put it there. Sometime during the party."

"It's a birthday card."

"Yes. Why don't you read it?"

Lambert took the card out of the envelope and read it. Then Shan saw his eyes darken and his lips thin.

"Birthday murderer," Shan said. "Someone is calling me a murderer."

"Yes," Lambert said softly.

"But why? I don't understand why."

Lambert still gazed at the card, and a puzzled look came into his eyes. "Shan, the handwriting on this card seems a bit familiar to me."

"It's mine," Shan said.

"Yours? Then I . . . Shan, I'm afraid I can't follow you."

"But, Paul, I didn't write that card."

"You just said it's your handwriting."

"I mean it's been copied."

"If this is someone's idea of a joke," Lambert said, "it's a very poor one."

"Is it a joke?"

"What else could it be?"

Shan took a deep breath and then spoke. "It could be true."

"Why do you say that?"

"I don't know," Shan said. "It just came to me."

"Just now?"

"Yes."

Shan knew that the man didn't believe him. He looked away from Lambert's piercing gaze to the people about him. Gradually he found himself catching wisps of talk, and he listened intently, trying to make sense out of the fragments. Then he heard Lambert's voice again.

"You found the envelope on your bureau?"

Shan turned back to him. "Yes."

"Propped up against your picture?"

Shan paled.

"Well, Shan?"

"How did you know that?" Shan almost whispered.

Lambert smiled. "Wouldn't that be the logical place for someone to put it?"

Shan nodded silently.

"The instant you entered the room you saw it, didn't you?"

"Yes."

Lambert smiled again. "So it was the logical place," he said.

"It was," Shan said slowly.

"And you saw no one go up the stairs during the party?"

"I didn't notice."

"But someone had to, if we are to believe that you didn't write the card. Isn't that so?"

"But I tell you, I didn't write the card, Paul."

"Yes. You did tell me that."

A bell sounded, sharp and insistent, and the people started to drift back into the theater. Shan caught a glimpse of his mother, standing at the other end of the lobby, watching them silently. He wondered how long she had been there.

"Paul," he said.

The man didn't seem to hear him.

"Paul, I know about the other birthday party."

Lambert raised his head sharply.

"I know that your son was burned to death."

The man flinched, and the agony came into his eyes.

"That's all I seem to remember," Shan said.

"Nothing else?"

"Nothing."

"Then let it be that way, Shan," Lambert said gently.

"It's over with?"

"Yes."

"Paul."

The man waited.

"Paul, am I a murderer?"

"What makes you ask such a question?"

"Am I?"

Lambert looked long at him. Then he said, "Why don't you ask your mother?"

Shan glanced down and away from the piercing eyes, and he saw that Lambert's hands were clenched tight. When he glanced up again, the man's face was smooth and impassive.

"Let's go back to the play, Shan," he said.

But Shan could not go back to the play. He sat in his seat, next to his mother and Paul Lambert, his eyes glued to the stage, but he saw nothing and heard nothing.

Am I a murderer, Paul?

VI

It was past midnight. He sat in the living room with his mother. Lambert had taken them home and left. The night had turned warm, and the windows were open. The lace curtains hung long and motionless. As he looked at them, he thought that in a way his mother was old-fashioned. She seemed to cling to the past. Now it seemed that the past was coming in, like deadly smoke, and choking the life out of him.

"What happened?" he asked suddenly.

They had been sitting silently, thinking separate thoughts.

"What, Mother?"

She turned with a sigh. "There was a birthday party."

"I know that," he said.

"Yes. You know that."

"Mother."

She looked away from his urgent gaze. He noticed that her hands were trembling. Her small, delicate hands.

"You were a child."

He came over to her.

"It wasn't your fault. It wasn't, Shan."

"Mother," he almost shouted. And then he controlled himself and said the word again, but this time low and quiet.

Her face was white and drawn. He could see the tiny wrinkles round her gentle eyes. She began to speak. "His son's name was George. And you adored him. You did, Shan. And he . . . he liked to play with you." She paused and then went on.

"Paul had invited us to the party. We went. And sometime before evening, George went up to his room. After a while, you got bored being with us and you followed him." She looked up at Shan. "Don't you remember?"

"No. No," he said fiercely. But in the pit of his stomach there was a cold, cold feeling. As if he did remember. Remember too well.

"You followed him upstairs. And then you played with him. And he got a bit tired and lay down on his bed."

"And then?"

She took a deep breath and went on. "He must've dozed off. There were some matches on the end table. You picked them up and began to play with them. You were only a child, Shan."

"I was five," he said.

She nodded. "Just five."

Outside a car passed; its sound floated up to them. They both paused, listening to it rigidly, as if both did not want to go on, but wished to lose themselves in the world that was outside the house.

She began to speak again. "Before that day, we had caught you a few times playing with matches. And once you had set a couch on fire." She shook her head vigorously before he could speak. "No, you were not a pyromaniac. No, don't think that. Don't. It was just a child playing with matches. The fascination of fire."

"Just that," he said in a low voice.

"Just that."

He wanted to laugh. He wanted to hear her say again, No, you were not a pyromaniac. For some reason, the word sounded absurd and ludicrous to him. A twisted smile hovered on his lips, but he did not laugh, for the cold, chilling feeling was still with him.

"You lit a match, and somehow the bed caught fire."

The smile fell away from his lips.

"You left the room and came downstairs."

She spoke in short, rapid sentences. Her eyes were focused away from him, as if seeing other images, from another time.

"I set the bed on fire?"

She didn't say anything.

"And then I left him there?"

She didn't seem to hear him. She began to speak again, and this time he could see that she was reliving the experience. Her voice was rapid and tense.

"You came downstairs. No one noticed you. We were

sitting, drinking and chatting. Paul Lambert was talking to your father. His wife had not come to the party. They had just been separated a short time before." She seemed to be out of breath, and paused an instant before going on again. "Paul was asking your father for advice. On how to get together with Nancy again. And suddenly we heard . . ." Her hands clenched, and then she bowed her head silently.

"You heard him screaming," Shan said.

Her shoulders shook.

"Tell me. Tell me," he said.

"I can't," she moaned.

"Where was I?"

"Let me alone, Shan."

He sat down at her side.

"Tell me. I want to know."

"You . . . were . . . standing next to Paul and your father."

"Just listening to them talk?"

She nodded.

"And I didn't realize what I had done?"

She didn't answer him. Instead, she reached her hand out to him.

"Mother," he said.

"No. You didn't. You didn't realize, Shan."

"Is that possible?"

"Yes, Shan." She gripped his hand. "You were only a child."

"That's right," he said bitterly. "Just a child."

The tears came down her cheeks. "You told us you had been playing with matches."

He got up and went to the window and looked

through the curtains out at the night street. And all he could see was the street light and the harsh, unyielding black outlines of parked cars.

"It was too late to save him?"

"He died in the hospital."

Shan winced and closed his eyes tight. The pain was hot and agonizing. Mother, Mother, if you love me don't tell me any more. Please don't.

Yet he heard himself ask, his eyes still closed, his face to the window: "Did he say anything?"

"Nothing. He never regained consciousness."

Shan slowly opened his eyes. He put his hand to them, and then let the hand drop hopelessly to his side. He turned to her almost pleadingly.

"He could have been smoking in bed and—" He saw the look of great pity on her face and stopped.

"He didn't smoke, Shan. Ever."

"But the matches."

She shook her head sadly. "They happened to be there. One of his friends may have left the matches. They were there."

"He was seventeen. Exactly seventeen."

"Yes," she whispered.

There was a stricken look on his face when he said, in a low, weary voice, "And so I am a murderer."

She rose swiftly and came to him. "Shan, you must never think that. Never."

He shook his head grimly. "What else can I think?"

"No. No. You were a child. You didn't know what you were doing."

"It seems that I did," he said, and his voice almost broke.

She reached her hands out desperately to him. "Shan. Shan, you were a child and you were innocent. Even Paul feels that way. He always did."

"Paul?"

"Yes. Yes. Isn't that clear to you? He understands fully. From the very first moment. Shan, he was heartbroken. We all were. But no one looks upon you as a . . . a . . ." Her voice trailed into silence.

"As a murderer?" he said.

"Don't say the word. Please."

"Mother, I—" he murmured and couldn't go on.

"Shan. Shan, if you'd only face this truth. That you are innocent."

"Am I?"

"Yes. Yes. Believe that and you will once and for all free yourself. All these years you've felt guilty. That's why you blocked out the memory. Your father and I knew this and we thought that if we left you alone, never questioned you once on what happened, you would work it out yourself, come to terms with it when you were ready to face it."

"And it seemed to be all right that way?"

"Yes."

"You never tried to get me any help?"

"You mean . . . a psychiatrist?"

He nodded.

"I wanted to. Right after it happened. I felt it would help you. But your father was strongly against it."

"Why?"

"He just didn't trust psychiatry. He felt it might do more harm than good to you then. He believed it best to leave you alone."

"And do you think it was?"

She didn't answer him.

"Do you?" he persisted.

"I don't know, Shan." She paused and then spoke again. "After your father died . . . I . . . You would tell me that you would see him sitting on the bench in the garden. Watching you while you played. It used to worry me greatly. I was thinking then of taking you to a psychiatrist. But you stopped seeing your father after a while."

"I sometimes still do see him, Mother," he said quietly. "But I haven't told you."

"Still?"

"Yes."

"You still see him?" she asked, her eyes now large and fearful.

"Clearly. Very clearly, Mother. It's been happening just recently."

A tremor went through her, and she touched his hand silently.

"Do you remember when I used to wake up during the night?" he asked.

"Thinking the house was on fire? Yes, Shan." She nodded and said again, "Yes. But it hasn't happened in years."

"It's beginning to happen again," he said. "But I didn't tell you." He heard the catch of her breath.

"Ever since Paul came back, you . . . you . . ." She didn't finish.

"Well?"

"You've been acting strangely."

"What do you mean?"

She now looked at him. "As if you suddenly . . . as if somehow . . . you remembered. All that had happened at that tragic party. And you felt guilty and fearful with him."

"Afraid of him?"

"I don't know how to explain it, Shan. But . . . I've discussed it with Paul, and he feels the same thing. That you shrink away from him at times."

"Because I killed his son."

"Shan, please . . ."

Shan took the birthday card out of his pocket. "And so I wrote myself this card. Calling myself a murderer."

She took the card and looked at it, her lips quivering.

"Well?" he asked.

"Shan, I don't know what to believe," she finally said.

"I didn't write the card."

"Then who did?"

"How the hell do I know?"

"Why should anyone write such a card to you? Why?"

"Dammit, I can't answer that!" he cried out. His mind was whirling; it was hard for him to think clearly.

"It's your handwriting. I can see that it is. Shan, I should know your handwriting by now, shouldn't I?"

He put the card back into his pocket and didn't answer her.

"I'm trying hard to believe you," she said. "So very hard."

"But you can't," he said.

She turned her agonized face away from him. "I don't know what to believe," she murmured.

He could hardly hear her voice, it was so low and choked with emotion. He went over to her and held her to him for an instant, and he wanted to cry to her, Help me, Help me, but he said nothing. He let her go and walked out of the room.

"Shan," she whispered.

She sat down on a chair, her hands motionless at her sides, and she stared into the past, for a long time.

VII

He sat on the stone bench in the garden. The night was quiet and seemed vast around him.

The windows of the house were dark. His mother had gone to her room, and he knew that she was in bed by now. He wondered if she could sleep, or if she too was reliving the past that had come back so relentlessly into their lives.

I don't know what to believe, Shan.

And he knew then that she could not sleep. That she was thinking, just as he was now. He looked down at his hand and saw the whiteness of the birthday card.

Happy Birthday, Murderer.

I did not write it!

His hand gripped the card, his face taut in the darkness. He sat there a long time, motionless, his mind whirling.

A slight breeze came up and rustled the branches above him. A few leaves fluttered in the darkness and fell at his side. He felt one brush his sleeve and linger an instant before falling away from him. The thought came to him that maybe he had written the card and then made himself forget. As I have done all these years. I'm pretty good at that.

His lips thinned in bitterness, but then he forced himself away from the thought. I didn't write it, he said to himself. I know I didn't.

Then who did?

And why?

Shan felt hot, stinging tears come to his eyes, and fiercely he brushed them away with his fist. Suddenly, savagely, he tore the card into bits and let the pieces drop to the dark grass at his feet.

"The hell with it all," he said grimly. "I won't think about it anymore. I'm through with it. Done with it."

The pieces of the card lay on the grass, and he could see their whiteness glimmering like little, dull stars; stars that lost their glitter—like his life.

Then he realized that it was no use to say the hell with it, for the thoughts forced their way back into his consciousness. They would not thrust aside, no matter how hard he tried. What if someone forged my handwriting? Someone who got hold of a sample and studied it and then wrote the card? Maybe it was Paul. He'd have every reason to send me a card like that. I killed his son. On the day of his seventeenth birthday, I killed him.

No. I can't believe Paul would . . . But I killed his son.

Shan got up from the bench, his face pale with agony. "I must not think this way. Can't let myself do it. Or I'll go—"

And it was at that moment that his eyes were drawn upward, directly to the windows of his room. He gasped. There by the front window was a figure, dark and motionless. In its hand was a burning candle; the flame glowed in the night.

Shan stood rigid.

Suddenly the hand that held the long, tapering candle moved closer to the lace curtain. The flame licked upward.

"Stop!" Shan cried out.

He ran desperately along the path that led out of the garden to the staircase that led into the house. He jammed open the front door and then rushed up the steps, his eyes wild with fear and urgency. His footsteps thudded and echoed through the silent house. He came to the landing, paused to catch his breath, and then dashed down the corridor. At the door to his room he stood stock-still. There was no one there. Absolutely no one.

His heart began to pound in his breast. He could swear that he could actually hear its rhythmical pounding. The sound became so loud that he wanted to scream. And all the while he stood looking at the empty, shadowy room.

"Shan!"

He slowly turned.

"Shan."

His mother was staring at him.

"There was someone in my room," he said.

She drew her robe about her, as if she had become very cold. Her lips quivered as she looked at him.

"I tell you, someone was here."

Still she didn't speak.

"About to set fire to the house."

"Fire?"

"Yes. Stood there by the window with a candle and—"

"What are you saying?" she cut him off desperately.

"There's someone in the house, Mother."

She shook her head and was silent. He had switched on the light, and now he could see the gray pallor of her face and the dark, terrified look in her eyes. And he knew that she was terrified of him and what was happening to him.

"You don't believe me."

She didn't answer him.

"I'm searching the rooms," he said. "Every one of them."

"Shan."

"I tell you, there's someone here."

She stood on the threshold, her shadow on the wall behind her. He expected to see another shadow slide along the wall at any moment and join hers.

"There's nobody here," she said.

"I saw him, I tell you." But he knew he wasn't sure.

"Who, Shan?"

He didn't know. He had seen only a figure, a dimly outlined figure.

"Well?"

He hesitated.

"Who?" she asked again.

"I couldn't see it clearly."

"It?"

He bit his lip and didn't speak.

"Shan, I've been awake all this time. I heard you running, I came out of my room and up the staircase. I saw no one come down it. I heard no one at any time. There is no one in the house."

But he had stopped listening to her. He turned and grabbed a baseball bat that stood in the corner of his room. "Dammit!" he shouted at her. "There is someone!"

He rushed past her and into the other room on the floor. Here he kept his hi-fi, his records and books. He switched on the light and gazed sharply around the room. He even went to his closet and opened the door. All the time he was aware of her, standing and watching him.

"No one," she said. "No one."

"No one," he echoed wildly. "No one."

He returned to his room and sat down heavily on his bed.

"Shan?" Her voice was small and plaintive.

"Leave me alone, Mother," he said.

But she stood there. "Please let me stay with you. Let's try to talk and work this out together. Please, Shan."

"I don't want to talk," he said, a dull and lost look in his eyes.

She was about to plead with him again, but she turned with despair and went out of the room. Her footsteps descended the staircase, and he heard her door close.

VIII

He put out the light and lay on his bed in the dark. He had not thought to take off his clothes. He just lay there, staring up at the ceiling. Someone had been in his room. Someone had stood by the garden window holding a candle, ready to set the house on fire. To pay back the birthday murderer. He was sure of it.

But was he?

Shan clenched his hands. Could it have been something he himself had created? A crazy hallucination?

"I saw it," Shan whispered fiercely, and then unclenched his hands almost hopelessly.

He lay there, his face a patch of glimmering white in the darkness, and soon he found himself thinking of his father. Remembering how the man had looked at him at times—an anxious, appraising look. As if he were trying to probe what was in his son's mind. The son who had already killed.

He was anxious about me, Shan thought. Full of fear. All the time. And now I know why. He was afraid that one day I would have a breakdown. And maybe set fire to someone else. Become a murderer again. And this time they'd put me away for good. Nobody would say he's only a child, a child that does not yet know what he has done.

Father, dear Father, the pain I must have caused you.

Shan got out of bed, went to the window, drew the curtain aside, and gazed down into the garden. It was quiet and serene. His eyes sought out the whiteness of the stone bench and sadly found it.

Now he felt himself a child again. He thought he could see the image of his father sitting on the bench. He yearned for it, wanted to go down and speak to his father, to be comforted by him. To once again feel the man's hand tenderly on his shoulder and to hear the soft, soothing, protecting voice . . .

But there was no one on the bench.

Shan sighed and slowly let the curtain fall.

"I saw it," he murmured to himself stubbornly. "I saw the candle and the flame. I know I did. If I didn't shout and rush up after him, he would've burned the house down. He got away somehow, but he was here. I'm sure he was here."

Suddenly Shan turned away from the window and put on the light. He gazed about the room, now bright and shining against the night. Somehow he felt a surge of hope spread through him, now that the darkness was driven out. There must be some marks, some clues . . .

He went over to his bureau and searched it carefully, but everything was in its place. Nothing had been touched. Then he walked to the window where the figure had stood, ready to set fire to the curtain. There should be some candle drippings here.

Shan studied the sill and then dropped to his knees and searched the floor for traces of wax. There were none.

He even crawled along the floor, hoping to find a burned-out match, anything that would give him proof that someone had been in the room. As he crawled along, he felt sure that if his mother were to come to the door and see him on his knees, she would think that he had cracked up at last, that he was past all hope.

He smiled at the thought. Yet as he rose to his feet, a haunting weariness came to his eyes. He sighed and shrugged his shoulders in futility. Then fear suddenly overwhelmed him, fear for his sanity, as he realized that there was not the slightest odor of burned wax in the room. Not even a lingering trace. Nothing.

"He was here. Dear God, please help me. Please . . ."

His voice whispered through the room and faded away. Shan went slowly to the light switch. Darkness flowed into the room.

He felt hopeless and desolate.

But sometime during the night, some hours later, after sheer weariness and despair had overcome him and he slept, a rustling sound filtered into his room. He woke and sat straight up in bed, all his senses taut and strained.

It was the sound of soft and stealthy footsteps going down the staircase, followed by the sound of the front door opening softly and closing.

Shan shivered and sprang out of bed. He hurried into the corridor and went along it to the front room. He stood by the window and peered out till his eyes caught the outlines of a figure swiftly disappearing into the thinning darkness.

He could not tell whether he was watching a man or a woman. He leaned forward, pressing his face to the cold glass. The figure blended into the darkness and was lost to his sight. I saw a man, he said to himself. It was a man's figure. I'm sure of that.

But when he was back in his shadowy room again, standing in a shimmering well of silence, he began to wonder if he had really heard the sounds and really seen the dim figure.

"I don't know anymore," he whispered. Then he stood stock-still and listened to the rustle of his voice fade away from him, like a ghostly echo.

He didn't sleep anymore that night.

IX

They sat across from each other at breakfast,
and for a while neither spoke. Her face had
a haggard look to it, and he knew that she
had not slept. You're starting to worry over me, Mother,
he said to himself. More than you have in years. You're
beginning to get frightened. Just as I am, Mother.
Frightened over what is happening to me.

He put down his half-empty cup of coffee. There was
no taste to it. His hands were shaking just a bit.

"Mother," he said.

She looked across at him.

"You're still upset over what happened last night,
aren't you? Just as I am."

She nodded and sighed. "There was no one in the
room, Shan. You know that, don't you?"

"There was no one," he said gently. "Let it be that way."

"But, Shan . . ."

"Why go into it, Mother? I don't know myself anymore what to believe."

They were silent for a moment. Outside the sky was gray and low.

"Tell me this," he said. "About four o'clock this morning. Were you asleep?"

She started. "Why do you ask, Shan?"

"Just tell me."

She seemed to think, and then she said, "I don't know. I slept fitfully. I may have been awake at that time. Yes, it's quite possible that I was awake. Why?"

He played with a paper napkin, his eyes fixed on it.

"Tell me, did you hear any footsteps?"

"Footsteps?"

"Down the staircase and then to the door." Now he looked at her and saw her eyes opened in horror. He went on. "The door opened and closed quietly. Very quietly."

"You say you heard all that, Shan?"

"Yes. And you?"

She shook her head and said nothing.

"I looked through the window, and I thought I saw someone going along the sidewalk, away from the house. Moving down the block. But I couldn't make out whether it was a man or a woman." He looked at her and said in a small, twisted voice, almost like a small boy, "Now that it's daylight I don't know whether I dreamed the whole thing or not."

"You did dream it, Shan," she said desperately. "You did."

"It seems so far from me now. So distant. I . . . I . . ." Shan played with the napkin and then fiercely crushed it in his fist. "I don't know, Mother," he said. "I don't know anymore. I don't."

He bowed his head.

"You dreamed it, Shan. You were very disturbed last night. You dreamed it." And she said it again, as if her constant repeating it would make it a fact, "You dreamed it. You did."

"I dreamed it," he murmured.

But when he was upstairs in his room again, alone, and he gazed up at the pattern of light and shade gliding along the pale ceiling, he said to himself, I did hear someone and I did see someone.

I did.

Suddenly he began to beat his fists on the wood of the desk, until he heard his mother's voice coming up to him, "Shan!" He stopped and sat down at the desk, not answering her. He knew that she was standing at the foot of the stairs, white and trembling.

Gradually, he became calm again.

X

In the afternoon of that day the sun broke through for a while, and everything became warm and pleasant. Shan sat on a bench in the park and idly watched some fellows playing touch football out on the wide swath of grass. He knew some of them, and he was about to join in the game when a man sat down at his side. It was Paul Lambert. Suddenly the day seemed to become cold and gray.

"Your mother said I might find you out here. She thought you might be playing."

"Not in the mood," Shan said.

Lambert sat back and gazed out at the field. Shan glanced at the lean, strong profile, and at the graying hair. The man wore a sweater and gray slacks. He looked young and trim.

"Your mother's worried about you," Lambert said quietly.

"So she asked you to come and speak to me."

"Yes."

"And what are you going to say?"

The ball sailed over a player's head and bounced along the ground until it came to a stop near them. Lambert got up, set the ball in his right hand, and threw a high, curving spiral. Shan watched the brown leather ball curve through the air gracefully and land in a player's hands. A perfect forward pass, he thought. Controlled it all the way in.

Lambert sat down again, a flush on his face. He was evidently pleased with what he had just done.

"Had a good arc to it," Shan said.

"Thanks."

"You ever play?" Shan asked.

Lambert nodded and smiled. "When I was much younger. For my college team."

"Varsity?"

"Yes."

Shan reached down and retied the loose laces of his sneakers. "What position?"

"End. I'm tall and rangy. Just right for it."

"Fast?"

"Sort of."

Shan straightened up and glanced appraisingly at Lambert. "I'll bet you did the hundred in about ten."

"Close to it." Lambert patted Shan on the knee. "Sometimes I broke ten."

"That's real fast. Even for today."

"Even for today," the man repeated softly.

"How many years did you play?"

"Three. I didn't play in my freshman year."

"Why?"

"Oh. Just happened that way." Then he said, "A car accident. I was hit by a drunk driver. Smashed me up. It was all his fault. I was crossing a street, the light was with me and . . ." Shan thought he could sense an edge of bitterness and hatred in the man's voice. Now he heard a gentle sigh. "Almost ruined my career."

"But it didn't."

"No. It didn't."

"What happened to the driver?"

"Why do you ask?"

"Just curious, Paul."

Lambert smiled and shrugged. His voice was pleasant. "Oh. I've long forgotten, Shan."

Yet Shan felt that the man was lying. He wanted to say to him, You paid the driver back. Somehow you got even with him. Because that's the kind of a man I think you are. Aren't you, Paul?

"Aren't you, Paul?" Shan said aloud.

"What?"

"Nothing," Shan said quickly. "Nothing."

A slight breeze came up and ruffled Shan's hair. He put his hand up to smooth it down again. "I'll bet you sometimes look back to your playing years," Shan said.

"I do, Shan."

Shan turned to him. "You are a man who looks back. Aren't you, Paul?"

The large gray eyes studied Shan. "At times, Shan. Only at times."

They were silent again. Lambert took out a pipe and

a pouch from his sweater pocket. Slowly, carefully, he filled the pipe, then lit a match. As Shan watched he thought of the figure at the window holding the flaming candle, then the flame tipping toward the lace curtain. Somehow the attitude of the hands was the same. He would swear it was.

He watched Lambert blow out the match and throw it away in the grass, and he thought of how he had got down on his knees in his room last night, seeking a burned-out match—something like this one.

"Have you always been an athlete, Paul?"

"Since my youth."

"And your son?"

For an instant Shan thought he saw a veil come over the man's eyes. The lips seemed to become hard and thin, but when Lambert spoke his voice was calm and pleasant. "Like me. Built somewhat like me." He puffed his pipe and gazed out ahead of him.

"Tall?"

Lambert nodded. "About your height, Shan."

"Was he a good athlete?"

"Yes. I had hoped he would play on the college team."

"How did he make out in high school?"

Lambert paused and then said, "He was All-State."

"He was good."

"Very good. The coaches were excited about him. Had quite a lot of offers for football scholarships." A slight tremor seemed to go through the man, but it passed so quickly that Shan wasn't sure it happened.

"But he chose the same college that you did."

"Yes. It was a matter of great pride and sentiment to

me. I felt that he was continuing a tradition. I had hoped that his son would do the same." He looked at Shan and smiled almost wistfully, and at that moment Shan felt very close to the man. "Kind of foolish, isn't it?" He nodded his head. "Yes, Shan. He was about to enter the University of Wisconsin. The same college, Shan, his father had attended. The very same."

"Just as I am about to enter Hamilton."

Lambert turned to him. "You plan to follow your father, don't you?"

Shan nodded. "He graduated from Hamilton."

"And then he went on to law school."

"Yes."

"And you plan the same?" The eyes were now studying Shan. Was there a trace of bitter sarcasm in them? Even more than that? Contempt?

"I hope to be a lawyer," Shan said.

"You'll make a good one, Shan."

"You think so?"

"Yes," he said, and Shan thought the man's voice had become soft and cutting. "A very good criminal lawyer."

Shan tried to fight away the chill that began to settle over him.

"Criminal?"

Lambert smiled. "Your father was one. Wasn't he?"

Shan shook his head. "He did very little of that."

Lambert reached over and patted Shan on the shoulder. "Oh. I forgot. That's true. He went in for civil practice."

Again Shan thought the man was mocking him. But he didn't say anything.

"He had very little to do with crime. That's true," Lambert murmured to himself. His face was lean and impassive.

But his son did, Shan thought. Isn't that what you mean?

They sat silently looking out at the players and watching the ball as it flashed in the autumn sun, flying like a sleek bird from one figure to another. The sky was clear and the air sharp and pleasant. The voices and the laughter of the players floated over to them.

"They seem to be having a good time out there," Lambert murmured.

"They always do."

And for an instant Shan wanted to get up and run away from the man and lose himself in the game. To forget, forget that there ever was a past. Christ, I had so much fun playing with the fellows. If I could only play again and never stop.

Lambert lit his pipe again. He held the flame over the bowl. "You ever play with them?"

"Many times."

"You're a bit of an athlete yourself, aren't you, Shan?"

Shan looked at him. "Nothing like you were, Paul."

Lambert tossed the match onto the grass. Shan watched it smolder and die.

"Or my son," Lambert said softly. "He would have been a great one."

Out on the field the players paused and seemed to idle awhile, resting. One of them held the ball up and beckoned Shan to join them. "Some other time," Shan called. He waved and smiled as he spoke.

"Why don't you join them?" Lambert asked quietly.

Shan turned and faced the man. "I'd rather sit here and listen to what you have to say."

"That's really what I came here for. To speak to you. Isn't that so?"

"That's right, Paul."

"We've been talking. Rather pleasantly, I thought."

Shan shook his head grimly. "I'm waiting, Paul."

Lambert puffed and then finally spoke. "'You have obsessions, Shan. And hallucinations. You are imagining things that never happened. You write a card condemning yourself as a murderer and then you forget that you did it."

"Did I write that card, Paul?"

"Is there any doubt about that?"

"Of course there is. I didn't write it. You know that I didn't. You sure do, Paul."

"I? How should I?"

Shan turned away from the man's direct gaze, and then he said in a low voice, "I don't know why I said that."

Out on the field the game started again, and the two sat watching. Then Lambert began to speak again.

"You still feel you didn't write that card, Shan. You forget and then you go about accusing others in your mind. I know that you do. Shan, any psychologist would be able to see that."

"What do you think it all means?"

Lambert didn't answer.

"Well, Paul?"

"We're very concerned about you," he said.

"You and Margaret."

"Your mother and I."

Shan smiled bitterly at him. "So I accuse others. And then I imagine someone trying to burn the house down. In fact, I see the person. And go through the house looking for him. Did Margaret discuss that with you?"

"Yes."

"Did she tell you I thought I heard someone leaving the house early this morning?"

"She did."

"It's all obsession, is that it? Hallucinations?"

"Yes."

"And it all goes back to my crime."

"Listen to me, Shan," Lambert said in a low and earnest voice. "You were a child when my son was taken from me. That is the only way to look at it. Believe me, that is the only way I ever looked at it."

"Is it?"

"Of course."

"And so you forgive me."

"There was never anything to forgive," Lambert said gently.

"Because I was a child."

Lambert nodded. "Exactly."

Shan's voice quickened. "And in a court of law a child is never guilty of any crime. Not even the crime of murder."

"That is so."

Shan leaned forward, his face taut. "But in your eyes, Paul?"

Lambert paled just a bit. "Innocent," he said.

"Are you sure?"

Lambert gestured almost harshly with his hand. "I'm a civilized man. What more can you ask of me?"

"That's true. You are civilized," Shan said.

"Then is there anything more to say on this subject?"

"Yes."

"What, Shan?"

"Why do you lie to me?" The words came out of Shan before he could stop them. They seemed to force themselves up from the very depths of his being.

Lambert's face darkened. He rose to his full height.

"Why?" Shan asked again.

"We'll talk another time, Shan. You're too keyed up now."

But Shan wasn't listening to the man. His voice rose as he said, "You don't forgive me. You don't. Just as I wouldn't forgive you if our positions were reversed. Isn't that so, Paul? Isn't it?"

Out on the field the players had stopped and were watching them.

"Liar. Liar!" Shan shouted.

And then stood there and watched the man turn and walk away from him.

XI

"I just lost my head, Donna," Shan said.
"Just started to shout at him."

"Shan."

They were sitting in the sculpture court of the Frick Museum. The water in the marble fountain in the center of the court murmured softly and endlessly. It was afternoon, and every now and then a few figures would saunter through, glancing around casually, and then Shan and Donna were alone again.

Shan looked across to the lean bronze statue of a winged angel, a statue that had been cast many centuries ago by a tortured man who lived in a cruel and tortured age. As he looked at it, absorbing its strange, magnetic beauty, he felt a brooding sense, dark and hopeless, a sense that the world, the entire world, in all its countless ages, was always gray and hopeless. That it was all futile.

"I just feel that he can never forgive me. Just feel it in my bones. Maybe that's why I started to call him a liar. I lost control. I shouldn't have. But I did. I did. Everything's falling apart at the center. I see things. I hear things. I find myself suspecting and fearing people. I don't sleep anymore. That's how it is, Donna." And then he said again, staring ahead at the blank marble wall, "That's how it is."

She sat there and let him speak. Just as she had when, on the subway, he had told her about the birthday party of so many years ago and the deadly fire he had started, the agony he had brought to so many people, and now to himself. Then he had told her about the birthday card on the bureau, the figure at the window, the footsteps on the staircase, and the dim figure disappearing into the morning distance. She had listened and had said but a few words, yet he knew by the press of her hand and the deep, sad look in her eyes that she understood the terror and the turmoil that were in him now.

He turned to her. "What's happening to me, Donna? I seem to be losing my grip on things. The past just seems to be coming in and overwhelming me. I remember reading once that one could never think the past out of existence. It can't be done. Nor can anyone ever really forget it. It's there, all the time, submerged inside. I tried to forget it. To block it out. But it's all coming back with a rush, and it's scaring the hell out of me. Mixing me up terribly. I . . . I just don't understand myself anymore . . . I don't make sense, do I?"

She took his hand and pressed it gently. The light falling through the high skylight filtered down on them, making her long, black hair sparkle and her lips glint softly.

The fountain murmured endlessly. All about them was an atmosphere of quiet and isolation.

"And I keep thinking of him. Of him. I just can't get Lambert out of my mind. I . . . I know I'm unfair to him, but I just don't like him and my mother being together. I think of my father and I . . ." He didn't go on.

"Your mother has a right to fall in love with him. And he with her. Your father has been dead a number of years, Shan."

"I know that."

"They're probably sleeping together. But why is that your business?"

"It isn't," he said. "And yet I'm jealous of him. That's a crazy thing to say, isn't it?"

"Not if that's the way you feel."

He looked away from her and seemed to be listening to the fountain, and then he said, "I just can't get him out of my mind. I keep saying to myself, what would I do if I were in his place?"

"What do you mean?"

"Dammit, I mean if he had killed my son. What would I do?"

"What would you do?"

He gazed into her clear eyes, and then he said, "I would try to understand and forgive. To . . . Ah, who the hell knows just what I would do?"

"You would do just that, Shan," she said. "And that's what he's done. He told you that it's all past and gone. That he considers you innocent. Isn't that so?"

"I know."

"So?"

"But can I believe him? Can I?"

"Why not?"

The fountain murmured softly in the hushed room, softly and inevitably. They both sat listening to it. And within he said to himself, Why can't I believe him? She's right. Why can't I?

"Why can't I?" he said aloud.

"Because you're letting the past get you all twisted up, Shan," she said in a low and earnest voice. "You just said it yourself, didn't you? That it's coming in and overwhelming you? Mixing you up so that you can't think straight anymore."

He didn't say anything. He leaned back against the glistening marble wall and let his eyes close. She's right, I can't think straight anymore. And yet I feel in my bones that the man has not forgiven me. That he's bitter and against me.

Then he heard her begin to speak again. "You say yourself you're beginning to fear and suspect. You see things, you hear things . . . Shan, you yourself don't even know whether you're imagining or actually seeing and experiencing. Isn't that so?"

Suddenly he felt a bitterness rise against her.

"So I wrote that card to myself. Is that it?"

Their eyes met, and then she said, "If you say you didn't write it, then I believe you, Shan."

"Then who did?"

She shook her head. "I can't answer you that. It's too puzzling."

"What if Lambert did?"

"Come on, Shan."

"What if he did?"

"You're reaching and you know it. Shan, come off it, will you?"

He looked away from her and over to the lean bronze statue and didn't speak. His clear-featured face had become tight and cold. "I didn't write the card. Goddammit, I'm sure of that. I would've remembered if I did."

"I said I believed you didn't write it."

He shook his head fiercely.

"No. No. Just like my mother. She doesn't know what to believe. And you're the same, Donna."

"Shan."

He grabbed her arm. "The same. The same." He felt his anger pouring out on her. His anger and bitter frustration. Because he really didn't know what to believe anymore. She flung his arm away from her.

"Shan, what the hell are you talking about? Now don't call me a liar, too. I just won't sit still for that. Cut it out, now."

He looked away from her blazing eyes and down at his hands. "I just said what I was feeling."

"Shan."

"That's really sick, isn't it?"

"When you call me a liar, yes," she said, her voice almost breaking. "It sure is, Shan."

He glanced up at her, and he knew that she was on the point of crying. He had never seen her cry, in all the years he had known her. He had gone to junior high with her and sat in the same class. It scared him, and he felt his hands tremble. I'll lose her, he said to himself. I'll force her away from me and then where will I be? Where, you damn fool?

"Let's get out of here," he said.

When they stepped outside the museum, the sun was shining in full brilliance.

"It's a lousy day," she said, without looking up.

She spoke hardly at all the rest of the time they were together.

XII

When he left her at her apartment house, darkness was beginning to fall. The whole afternoon and evening had been a bust. He had hurt her, but he had hurt himself more, and he bitterly realized it as he began to walk the long blocks to his home. I'm scared. I'll have no one to turn to. My mother looks at me with fear and bewilderment in her eyes. All the time. I know it. She doesn't know how to handle what's happening to me. I don't even know myself. So how the hell can I blame her? I'm surrounding myself with fear. And there's fear inside me.

Shan paused at an intersection and stood motionless, watching a bus pass by. A slight wind had come up, and he felt chilled. He turned up his coat collar and watched the bus, lit and almost empty, swiftly lose itself in the gathering darkness, its lights and form suddenly blotted out.

As if it had never been, he thought to himself. That's how it is with death—it just blows you away and you're gone. You light a match and you're through. Just like that. One strike of the match and someone starts screaming. And even after he stops screaming, you hear it inside you, even if you think you don't; you hear it all the same, all the while, your entire life.

He crossed the intersection, his head down, his hands thrust into his pockets. Finally he turned down a tree-lined street that had a diner at its end. He went into the diner and sat down at the counter and ordered a cup of coffee. The place was warm and cozy; he always liked coming here with Donna and some of their friends, just to sit away the time and talk, but now there were only two other people there. He felt cold and isolated, and he wanted to warm himself within, to talk to someone.

"Not much doing," he said to the counterman.

"This is the dead time."

"Yeah. I know."

The counterman was strange to Shan; he had never seen him in the place before.

"Later on the place gets lively. Another hour or so."

Shan nodded. "The place will be jumping."

"I wouldn't say that. Just lively."

"You don't like that."

The counterman grinned. He was a lean and sallow man. "If I owned the place I would. But I don't. I'm just a fill-in."

"I never saw you here before."

"And you won't again."

There was no more talk. Shan glanced through the

store window and out into the street. Just where the circle of light ended and the darkness began, there on the other side of the street, he thought he could see a figure in the dark, leaning against the elm tree. It reminded him with a cold shock of recognition of the figure he had seen disappearing down the early-morning street.

Shan stood up, and it seemed to him that he could hear again the footsteps going down the staircase and then the door opening and shutting. He strained his eyes as the figure moved away and merged into the night.

"What's the matter?" the counterman asked.

Shan turned back to him. "Just thought I saw somebody I knew."

"You don't seem to be too happy about it."

"I guess I'm not," Shan said.

The counterman looked at him sharply and then moved off. Shan sat down on the stool again and began drinking his coffee. The figure seemed familiar to him. It shimmered in and out of his consciousness, and all the while he strove to identify it.

I know who it is. I know.

The two people got up and left the diner, and now Shan was alone with the counterman. A heavy stillness settled over the place. Shan looked up from his coffee and watched the man shine the large coffee urn.

The sharp ring of the telephone knifed through the stillness. The counterman dropped his rag on the counter and went to the telephone booth.

"Hello? . . . Who?"

He turned and looked over to Shan. "You Shan Rourke?"

Shan felt himself tremble.

"Are you?"

"Yes."

"There's a phone for you."

"For me?"

"That's right."

Shan got off the stool and went into the phone booth and closed the door.

"Hello?"

"Shan?"

It was a man's voice, but a voice he had never heard before. It had a low, whispering quality to it. It made his flesh creep.

"Yes?" he asked.

"Should a murderer be allowed to live?"

"What?"

"Or should he be executed?"

"Who are you?"

"Answer the question, Shan."

"Lambert?"

But he wasn't sure the voice was Lambert's.

"Answer it, Shan," the voice whispered, and then it rustled into silence.

"What do you want of me? What?"

"A death for a death."

There was a click, and a humming, ringing silence enveloped Shan. He felt faint. His knees began to buckle, but he grabbed against the sides of the booth and gradually drew himself upright.

When he got out of the booth he was white and bathed with sweat. He paid for his coffee and without a word went outside into the darkness of the night.

XIII

Shan paused under a street light, his face taut with triumph and anxiety. So I was right, he thought to himself. I imagined nothing. It all happened: the figure at the window, the burning candle, the footsteps, the card—even the card. It happened.

He walked away from the light and into the darkness again. The sidewalk stretched along the rim of the park. The wind had come up, and the branches of the trees rattled. But he heard nothing and saw nothing. He didn't even look up to see the leaves rustling and shaking above him. His head was down, his hands clenched at his sides. He passed the dark bulk of a park toolshed, and when he was no more than a hundred feet from it he heard a *whish* and then something small and hard almost grazed his arm and thudded into the bark of a tree behind him. Shan stood stock-still and peered breathlessly ahead of him. There, just barely outside the rim of the next light, was the dark figure he had seen outside the diner, and now he could make out the glint of a gun barrel.

"Christ help me," he whispered.

He turned and ran desperately for the cover of the small woods that began behind the repair shed. He heard the *whish* again; this time the bullet went over his head and on into the night. Shan ran headlong into the cluster of trees, his heart pounding in his chest, his breath coming in sharp gasps. He ran wildly, crashing into bushes and trees, a hunted animal in panic. He burst into a clearing and ran through it till he found the shelter of another cluster of trees. Finally he could go no farther. He staggered to a halt and leaned against the trunk of a huge tree, desperately trying to regain his breath. There was nothing now but a vast silence and the sound of the wind soughing through the trees.

Who is it? Is it Lambert? I don't know, but whoever it is, he's out to kill me. Shan listened intently for the sound of a pursuer. But he heard nothing. Not even the slightest rustle. Only the wind. The constant wind.

He began to think that the man had not followed him, when suddenly there was the *whish* and the thud of a bullet against a large boulder.

"Lambert! Let me alone!"

There was no other sound. Nothing but the cry of his voice, like that of a fearful and lost child. Crying for pity. And he knew there would be no pity. That it was useless to plead for his life.

He turned and ran in the direction of the park lake. He could see it faintly gleaming in the far distance. For some reason that had an absurd logic to it, he felt that if he could reach the lake he would be saved. The water would save him. Just get his body into the water and sink under it and he would never be hurt again. He would live forever, submerged in the water of the lake. His eyes yearned for the lake, his whole being, while his breath came in hot gasps, burning like a fiery knife in his chest. The lake was getting closer and closer when his foot caught in a root and he fell headlong, hard. The lake vanished from his sight. He lay on the ground, stunned, his eyes closed, his mouth open wide.

Yet he was still aware of the danger. Still aware of the lake gleaming in the night, so close to him, so very close. Back in the innermost recesses of his mind and being, he knew that he must get up again. Get up and run some more. Run till he plunged his hot body into the cold waters of the lake. You must save your life. You must. Shan!

He lay there, powerless to move. Desperate thoughts rolled over him, like a great gray fog. His face against the cold earth. Over him, the wind blew.

When he came to, he knew that the man was standing at the edge of the clearing, looking down at him. Shan did not turn his head to see, but lay there, waiting—waiting for his death.

Then he heard the slow approach of the man.

The pause.

The gun barrel, cold and icy against his temple.

The pause.

Then the slow withdrawal of the gun barrel from his temple. The steps retreating to the edge of the clearing.

The pause.

Then the sudden high-pitched peal of laughter that was more terrifying than the gun.

Then the laughter disappeared into the windy night.

XIV

There was a decanter of wine standing on the bar in the living room. He poured himself a glass and drank it down. Then he stood there, still trembling, feeling that he would never get warm again, that the deadly chill would never leave him. His hand gripped the neck of the decanter, and as it did he murmured, "Father," and wished with all his soul that his dead father would come to life and stand next to him, warm and alive, and put his arm about him and say, "No one is going to harm my son. No one." And then he would take the bottle away from Shan, set it back in its place on the bar, and say, "This is my decanter, Shan. It was given to me by my father. I once told you that, didn't I? And I said that in time you will give it to your son. You're going to live, Shan. You will. No one is going to kill you. Believe me. No one."

The phone rang and startled Shan. The decanter almost slipped from his hand to the floor, but he caught it in time and set it back on the bar and stood listening to the clear, cold ringing. It stopped and then began again. Finally he grabbed up the decanter and went over to the phone and picked up the receiver.

"Shan?"

It was his mother.

"Yes?"

"I've been trying to get you."

"I just got in," he said, and he wanted to add, I ran all the way, Mother. Ran all the way home, like a scared, fearful child. I didn't stop once, not even once, just ran and ran till I got in the house and locked the door behind me. The wine was beginning to warm him. He put the bottle to his lips and let the wine roll on his tongue and then down, spreading itself throughout his body. But the inner fear and chill would not leave him.

It was Lambert and he wanted to kill me. Who else could it be? Dammit, it was Paul Lambert.

"I wanted to know how you are."

"I'm okay," he said.

What's the use of telling her? Would she believe me? Maybe I should. Maybe I should try her? Why not try her? She's my mother, dammit. My mother.

"Did you have a good time with Donna?"

"Yes," he said.

He drank again from the bottle, but the deadly chill would not leave him.

"I just saw a friend of yours," he said.

"A friend? Who?"

"Paul. Paul Lambert."

"Where?"

"Out in the park."

"But, Shan, I just spoke to Paul. He's at home, in his apartment."

"Did you see him?"

"No. I spoke to him on the phone."

"Did he call you or you call him?"

"Shan."

"Well?"

"Shan, I'm waiting for him in the lobby of the Hilton. He called to say he was delayed and will soon be here."

"He's a liar."

"Shan."

"He was in the park. Just fifteen minutes ago."

"But I tell you—"

"He tried to kill me, Mother."

He heard her gasp. There was a pause. He listened for an instant to someone walking out on the sidewalk. The footsteps sounded sharp and urgent in the stillness. Then they were gone, and the silence enveloped him again.

"I said he tried to kill me, Mother. But then he decided not to. I guess he wants me to suffer some more before he—"

"Shan," she cut in desperately. "Shan, please get hold of yourself. I tell you, I just spoke to Paul."

"Oh, who can believe anybody anymore," he said bitterly.

"Shan."

"The hell with you all!" he shouted and slammed down the phone. He walked away from it to the window and stood staring out into the night. He felt that somewhere, not too far away, Lambert was standing and laughing silently. His eyes cold and deadly.

"Maybe it wasn't Lambert. Maybe she's right. Maybe the whole thing never happened to me. Maybe I'm . . . just going out of my head."

The phone rang again, insistently. He let it ring; he did not want to speak to her. He just wanted to be left alone. He put the bottle to his lips and drank again, and then he sat down heavily in one of the chairs.

The phone began to ring again. Shan chuckled to himself, and this time he got up and went over to it, and as he walked he spoke aloud to the room. "The hell with it. Let's hear what she has to say. It should be good. One should always listen to what mothers say. Isn't that so?"

He picked up the phone and it fell out of his hand. He stooped and picked it up again and put the mouth-piece to his ear and the earpiece to his mouth. "Hello. Hello!" he shouted. Then he chuckled, and jammed the receiver back onto the cradle. He stood there grinning and swaying just a bit. The phone began to ring again. He picked it up, and this time he got it right.

"Go ahead," he said with a laugh.

"Hello, Shan."

It was the whispering voice that he had heard in the diner, but now he was able to recognize it. Shan stood there, breathing heavily.

"Sleep well. Tomorrow is another day."

Then he heard the laughter, the high-pitched laughter, and it chilled the wine out of his system and he was cold and trembling again.

The voice was that of Paul Lambert. This time he was sure of it.

XV

When he came into his room toward evening of the next day, the letter was waiting for him. It was propped up on his bureau, white and gleaming, and it made him think of the birthday card. His face paled as he picked up the sealed envelope. There was no name or address of the sender, and the postmark was New York, N.Y.

He opened the envelope and drew out the letter. Then he sat down on a chair and read it.

Dear Shannon Rourke,

Perhaps the time has come to explain our relationship to each other. I consider you a murderer and I consider myself your appointed executioner.

Simple enough, isn't it?

Shan breathed in deeply and read on.

Have you a dictionary at hand? Of course you do. Open it to the page on which the word *monomania* is defined. Now read the definition along with me. *Monomania*, insanity in which the patient is irrational on one subject only.

Now I do not consider myself insane, nor am I a patient in a mental institution. But I am certainly irrational when I deal with you and the death of my only son. I even get a savage pleasure in being irrational when it concerns you, my young friend. There is another part of the definition. Read that, too. Here we are. Excessive concentration on a single object or idea.

There again, I find the definition quite accurate. All the years since the fire, all the long hours, all the minutes, I have thought but one thought, Shannon Rourke. How to pay you back for what you did to my life. Do you know that you even destroyed my marriage? That my beloved wife would have made up with me, but after the murder she refused to have anything more to do with me? She accused me of being criminally negligent. Maintained bitterly that I could have prevented the death of our son. What do you think of that, my young arsonist? Is she right? Of course not. You know better than anybody else in this world that nothing, absolutely nothing, ever stops a murderer. Isn't that so? Of course it is.

So, Shannon Rourke, we now stand naked and revealed to each other,

Till your inevitable death,
Paul Lambert

The entire letter was written by pen, in a handwriting that Shan instantly recognized. It was his own.

Shan took out a pen and sheet of paper and carefully copied every word of the letter. When he was done he compared the two letters. They were identical.

"It can't be," he whispered.

Shan went out of the room and waited for a few moments in the hallway, as an icy fear settled over him.

Finally he went back into his room and approached the two sheets of paper. He had placed them face down on his bureau. The copy was folded like the letter. He stood there quietly. The evening was just coming in, and the daylight was now thin and cold, yet streaked with a pinkish flush. The sheets of paper glowed.

He picked up one and began to read it, and a cold horror swept over him. He could not tell which was the original and which was the copy.

"Christ," he whispered to himself.

Then he knew that Lambert had spent years studying his handwriting. Somehow he had got hold of specimens and copied them endlessly.

Like a monomaniac.

Till it was impossible to tell the difference between his handwriting and Shan's. Not even an expert could, Shan thought hopelessly.

He stared at the two letters. They're so damned identical. How could . . . ? And suddenly Shan remembered he had argued with his mother over a school notebook that he couldn't find. It had just disappeared from his room. She had maintained that he had left it at school. But he never found it again.

It was all coming back to him. He was older now, in his junior year at high school. He had been out in the park, playing baseball with some friends. He had come home and gone up to his room. No one else was in the house. He began taking off his jersey, and then suddenly stopped and stared about him. Something was wrong. Somebody had been in his room. He was sure of that. It was an uncanny, weird sensation. Shan started to search about the room, to see if anything was missing. But everything was in its place. Then he went downstairs and searched all over.

It was only some weeks later that he noticed, almost casually, that two term papers were missing from his desk. He had gotten excellent marks for them and wanted to keep them.

He never found them again.

Then there was the batch of letters and postcards he had sent to his mother when he was away on a summer camping trip. She liked them so much (You write extremely well, Shan. It was a delight to read them) that she kept them on her dresser in her room. And they, too, were lost.

Did you take them, Shan?

Why should I take them?

And she had flushed and murmured apologetically, I don't know why I asked you that. I really don't.

Because sometimes I do strange things, Mother, he said.

But she didn't answer him.

Now all these disappearances fell into a pattern. One way or another that monomaniac Lambert had been able to get samples of his writing. He had come back here from the coast and gotten into the house when nobody was around. Like a thief. Leave it to him. That bastard could do anything. He's crazy enough.

Shan stood looking at the two letters.

If I showed this letter to anybody else, who would believe I didn't write it? Would Donna? Would my mother?

He shook his head bitterly.

They wouldn't. No matter how hard I tried to convince them. Even if I tried to show them how Lambert has been stealing samples of my writing over the years. Hell, how could I blame them for not believing me? He's been too smooth. What proof have I? Things have disappeared. As Donna would say, I've lost things, too, Shan. Misplaced them all over the place. We all do. You can make a pattern out of anything if you really set yourself to it. Isn't that so? You suspect somebody and it's damn easy to build a case. If you really want to. Just look how people build a case against a minority. Against the blacks, for instance. You know the whole deal, Shan. We've discussed it many times, haven't we? You know it, Shan.

Yes, Donna. I know.

Where are your facts? Hard facts, Shan.

I have none.

So?

I'm boxed in, Donna. The bastard's too smooth.

Shan took the two letters and savagely tore them into bits. He stood a long time gazing down at the white scraps of paper, his breath coming in short gasps. Then he said to himself, I'm going to crack up before this is over. Or maybe I'll kill him first.

XVI

From where they sat in the car they could see the light on in Shan's room, then the shadow of his form as it passed the shaded window. The rest of the house was in darkness. It was close to midnight, and the street was quiet and empty, except for the looming forms of the parked cars.

"I'm getting very anxious about him, Paul," Margaret Rourke said.

Lambert gently patted her hand. "I know you are, Margaret. I am too."

He sighed and took out his pipe, filled it with tobacco, and then struck a match. The flame showed the sharp, strong features of his face, the large brooding eyes. Then the darkness closed in again. They were parked just a little away from the circle of the street light.

Soon she would leave him and go into the house. They had been to an Artur Rubinstein concert at Carnegie Hall, and all the time she was there she had not thought of Shan. Not for an instant. The music and the evening were too enveloping. But now that they were back in front of the house, her fears and anxieties broke through, and the night seemed to her a waste. She even felt guilty for enjoying herself, as if in a way she had betrayed Shan.

"I don't know if he's well, Paul. I've begun to think that," she said.

"Perhaps it was all a mistake my coming back east," he said thoughtfully.

She turned to him. "No, Paul. Don't say that. Please."

He smiled gently but sadly at her. "I know how you feel, Margaret. But I . . ." He moved his large hands expressively and was silent.

"I'm glad you came back," she said simply.

He leaned forward and kissed her hair gently. "I know."

"I've been very lonely all these years."

"I have too," he said.

She rested her head on his shoulder and they were silent. He smoked quietly, his face a calm mask.

"He worries me so," she said. "I'm getting frightened, Paul. I can't sleep anymore. I . . ."

Lambert looked ahead of him into the darkness of the night.

"I couldn't understand what he was saying last night, Paul. I just couldn't. I tried to speak to him today, but he avoided me all the time. I keep going over it again and again."

"When you phoned him?"

"Yes." She had moved away from him. The anxiety had gripped her again. "The way he questioned me. It was so odd. Almost terrifying."

Lambert nodded. "He wanted to know where I was, Margaret. He's positively obsessed with me. I seem to be in his thoughts all the time."

"He wouldn't believe that you were in your apartment."

"But I was." Lambert puffed thoughtfully. A glint of a smile flashed in his eyes. Then it swiftly vanished. "I was," he said again. "Until I left to meet you."

"I know, Paul. But he said that you were in the park. I felt myself go cold all over when I heard him say that."

Lambert sighed. "Yes."

"He spoke as if he had seen you and talked to you."

"It's quite possible that he thought he did. Considering the feverish state of his mind."

She drew in her breath. "That you tried to kill him. It was eerie, Paul, positively eerie—and heartbreaking."

"It is, Margaret."

"Paul, he's normal about everything else. But when it . . ." She didn't finish.

"Only when it comes to me," he said. "Then he loses his grip on things. Isn't that so, Margaret?"

She nodded silently.

"I understand it fully." Lambert paused, his eyes veiled. "There's a word for it, Margaret. It's called monomania. Rational on every little thing in life but one." His voice rose just a bit. "But one, Margaret.

That's monomania." Now his voice lowered almost to a whisper. "Monomania, Margaret."

"On one subject."

"One. When it grabs hold of you, you are powerless. It simply floods your mind. Your being. You think of nothing else."

He struck a match and relit his pipe. His face was harsh and stricken in the flickering flame, like an ancient mask; the eyes peering through it were harsh and deadly. But she did not see it. She had turned to look at the lit window again.

"It's guilt, Margaret," he said after a while. "Guilt for the past."

She turned back to him. "The past?"

"Yes. Shan will not forget it, because underneath it all he doesn't want to."

"Why?"

"Because he wants to punish himself again and again for what he has done. A crime should be punished. That's his only way of coping with his agonizing sense of guilt."

A car passed, and they watched it go down the block to the corner and then gradually disappear, its red taillights sinking into the night.

Lambert spoke. "Whatever you might say, my coming back into his life was a bitter mistake. I was foolish, extremely foolish about it. Almost criminal. As a psychologist I should've known better. But this always happens when we lose our perspective. I lost mine. Because I grew to care so much about you. Margaret, I never should have come back."

"No, Paul."

He shook his head sadly. "I had hoped that everything would turn out for the best. But it hasn't. You know it hasn't."

She leaned forward to him. "It will. I'm sure it will."

"Are you?"

She didn't speak.

"I wanted to show him that the past was gone forever. I felt a duty to him, and to you."

"I know, Paul."

"I also didn't realize that when I saw you again I'd . . ." He paused and didn't go on.

"I didn't either," she said.

"Was it our loneliness?"

She drew closer to him. "With me it's more, much more than that, Paul."

"Are you sure, Margaret?"

"Very."

"It's the same with me," he said. He kissed her, then gradually drew away. "We have to help him. For our sakes. And his, Margaret."

"Yes, Paul."

"Shan should be seeing a psychiatrist."

She turned to him. "I've thought about that constantly. But how can we get him to go to one?"

"It will be difficult. It's clear he won't go on his own," he said thoughtfully.

"You know he won't. Particularly if I asked him to. Earlier tonight when I called, he slammed the phone down. He sometimes acts as if I've become his enemy. I can feel it. I—"

"It's not wise that you should suggest his going. You'd get a violent reaction." He puffed and then said, "How about Donna?"

"I've thought about that, too."

"Well?"

"I know she's very concerned about him."

"Good."

"Maybe she can persuade him to go."

"It's worth a try, isn't it?"

They sat silently, thinking. The small street stretched out before them, desolate, like a stage set of a tragedy, waiting for the actors to appear and the dark play to begin.

Upstairs in the house, Shan stood by the window and looked down into the street, his eyes seeing darkness and pools of lamplight, nothing more.

He turned away and went over to his desk and sat down. The scraps of the letters that he had torn that evening still lay scattered on the floor about him. The clock on the bureau ticked in the silence.

He found himself concentrating on the sound, following its inexorable rhythm, till the sound entered and filled his whole being. It grew louder and louder, TICK-TOCK, TICK-TOCK, until he thrust his hands to his ears and was about to let out a piercing scream. Then the sound began to recede, to become lower and lower, until he heard it no more. But it began again, tick-tock . . . This time it stayed low and bearable.

He breathed out slowly, and as he did he thought to himself, before this is over one of us will be dead. Who knows which one it will be?

He got up and went restlessly to the window again and looked down into the street, as if somewhere down there was a way out of the trap. His eyes focused on the bulk of a parked car. But his mind was far, far away, lost in the labyrinth of its own inner world. I never had a chance, he said to himself. I was jinxed from the very beginning.

He pulled down the shade and left the window.

"Shall I phone Donna or try to see her?" Margaret asked.

"I think it best if you saw her."

"Away from the house."

"Of course."

"All right. I'll call her the first thing in the morning."

Lambert nodded. "But don't alarm her. Just say you think it best that he go for a session or two, just to get back his perspective on things."

They were silent.

"Paul," she said.

"Yes?"

"Shan might turn against her. He might look upon it as a betrayal. And then he would lose her as a friend."

"It's a chance we have to take, Margaret."

"He'd feel completely alone. Abandoned."

Lambert didn't speak. His lips thinned a bit.

"Yes," she finally said, in a sad, trembling voice, "there's no other way."

"There is none."

Soon he held her in his arms and kissed her. The light in the room upstairs went out, and the house was completely dark.

XVII

Shan slept fitfully that night. He got up a few times and stood by the window, gazing down into the garden, his eyes seeking out the stone bench. Once he thought he saw his father sitting there, his cigar glowing in the darkness. Shan strained forward with his very soul, and now he could make out the outlines of his father's beloved face and the gleam of his eyes. Then Shan thought he could see the filmy shape of his mother come through the bushes and stop by the bench and gracefully sit down next to the shape of his father. The two parents sat close to each other—his father's strong arm tight about the narrow waist of his delicate mother—their eyes lifted upward, appraising Shan, ever appraising him. Just as he was about to cry down to them for help, the very instant his lips opened to shout, Save me, please, please!, the figures shimmered and dissolved away into the night.

They've abandoned me, he said to himself. They gave up on me a long, long time ago. And I'm alone. So damned alone.

In the morning, Shan got out of the house and walked in the park, walked through the mists, and watched the early dew glinting on the blades of the grass, watched till it slowly dried with the coming of the sun. He walked for hours, roaming about, his eyes vacant and absorbed. When he got back to the house, he was still tense and abstracted.

It was like fighting smoke, and it was making him desperate. He didn't know how to handle it, what to do about it. To whom to turn. He felt so alone, so bitterly alone. When Donna called him early that afternoon, he was glad to hear her voice.

"Hello, Shan."

"Donna."

"Doing anything tonight?"

"Nothing in particular."

"Want to do something?"

"What are you offering?"

"Gennaro."

"Gennaro?"

He felt something awaken and walk through the shadows of his mind. A memory. A glowing memory.

"The Feast of Saint Gennaro. How about it?" Donna asked.

"You mean in the Village?"

"That's right."

They had gone there last year and had a good time. But that was last year, an eternity ago.

"How about it, Shan?"

He hesitated.

"Come on, Shan. I've had three offers already. And I've turned them down."

He began to smile. "Three?"

"That's right."

"Well, you're a pretty girl. Why shouldn't you have three? Or was it four?"

"Could be. So?"

He was smiling, but still he hesitated. And he didn't know why.

"I'd really like to go, Shan." Her voice was now earnest.

"Uh-huh."

"With you. Well?"

"Just thinking."

"Do you have to think so hard? I'm insulted."

Suddenly he knew why he was hesitating. He didn't trust her. He didn't trust anybody anymore. The thought shocked him.

"Okay, Donna," he said.

Now he knew how much Lambert had gotten to him. That he should turn away from Donna—even from her.

I'm going nuts. And as he said that to himself, the words of a song he had heard at a concert a long time ago flashed into his being.

> *The animals of the street*
> *Have joined the animals of my mind*
> *And I'm goin' mad,*
> *I'm goin' mad*

"When do you want to go, Shan?"

He shivered and then said, "Any time you want, Donna." His voice was now gentle with her.

"How about six thirty?"

"You've got a deal."

"So why did it take so long?" She laughed.

"I was playing hard to get." He smiled.

"But all the time you wanted to go?"

"Sure."

She laughed. "Can't understand you these days, Shan."

"That makes two of us, Donna." He laughed again.

There was a pause, just for an instant, and in that pause his distrust began to return. He fought it down.

The words of the song jangled in his mind and vanished as he heard her voice again.

"See you at Prospect Park station. Okay, Shan?"

"Six thirty sharp. Don't eat. We'll pick up stuff at the stands as we walk along."

"Bring money."

"You too."

She laughed. His eyes lit up as he listened to her laughter.

"So long, Shan."

" 'Bye, Donna."

He waited for the click and then he hung up. He sat there for a while, feeling her warmth and buoyancy, and he knew how much he cared for her, how much he truly needed her. Gradually he became aware of his mother standing behind him. He turned and saw her at the threshold of the room.

"Was that Donna?" she asked.

"Yes."

"How is she?"

"Fine."

"I haven't seen her for days."

Somehow he felt that she was lying to him. But then he realized that he didn't trust her anymore, so he attributed the thought to that. "She's been busy."

"Are you going to see her?"

He nodded, his eyes trying to search her. "Tonight," he said.

Her face seemed to brighten. So it appeared to him, but he couldn't be sure.

"Have a good time, Shan."

He watched her leave and merge into the dimness of the house.

I'm going to end up hating her, he thought. Because somewhere along the line she has betrayed me. To him.

His face became tortured and hard, but his eyes were cold and agonized. Like Lambert's.

The words of the song came back to him, and now the tune began, precise and clear. It danced in his mind again and again.

> . . . *animals of my mind*
> *I'm goin' mad*
> *I'm goin' mad*
> *I'm goin' mad*

He felt the tears trickling down his cheeks. He bowed his head and closed his eyes.

I'm going mad.

XVIII

As Shan walked with Donna through the crowds, an old feeling swept over him. It was as if they were back at San Gennaro a year ago, before Paul Lambert had come on stage again. Yes, that was it. It was Lambert's return that had done all the damage.

"Having a good time?" he asked.

"Yes, Shan."

"Same as last year?"

"Even better."

"Okay." He smiled. "Good!"

It was the lights, the noise of the happy people about them, the lusty shouts of the barkers, the spin and whirr of the gaming wheels, the constant, unconquerable music that was like a tide, the flow of people up and down the wide stone staircase of the old, simple church, the wooden doors opened wide . . .

"It's a festival of life, isn't it? Of hope, Donna."

Death is far away from us now, Donna. Death and fear and madness.

"Makes you feel better, doesn't it?" he asked.

She looked at him and pressed closer to his side. "That's a good way of putting it, Shan."

He nodded, his eyes sparkling. "Makes you forget everything."

"Yes," she murmured, staring up at him.

"Almost makes you want to sing out loud."

He stood there, tall and fair and handsome. There was a golden glow about him. At that moment, to her, he looked like a young Viking, ready for any adventure life had to fling at him. She thought of the words his mother had said to her that morning as they sat in the restaurant. He needs a psychiatrist, Donna. Needs one badly. He's on the verge of cracking up. You're aware of it too, aren't you, Donna?

Donna looked at Shan now and she wanted to cry out, But he's a Viking. Can't you see it? Can't you? Tears almost sprang to her eyes.

Shan had turned to her and was speaking.

"People should always enjoy themselves," he said to her, his voice full and strong. "They look best when they're smiling and loving each other. They really become so beautiful. The other way they're like animals. They talk and act like savage animals, and start to look like them. That's when they go the other road." He stood tall and gazed about, his eyes soft and loving. "But this way," he murmured, "they're beautiful."

She reached up and touched a lock of his hair.

"You know, Shan, you said that last year."

"I did?"

She laughed tenderly. "Almost word for word."

"And you remembered?"

"Yes."

He smiled and put his arm around her. "I haven't felt that way for a long time," he said.

She nodded slowly. "You haven't, Shan."

They began to walk again.

"Some zeppoles?" he asked.

"Still have room?"

"You?"

"I always have room for zeppoles."

"Whose turn to buy?"

"Yours. I bought the clams."

"I forgot."

"That's what you say."

He laughed and bought a bag of zeppoles, and they pushed their way through to a tenement stoop, went up a few crowded steps, and found a spot for themselves at the top. They sat close to each other, eating and listening to an old Abruzzi folk song coming from one of the loudspeakers near them. It was a love song with a sad and poignant melody. A singer on the sidewalk took up the melody and sang from the loneliness of his soul, and even though they did not understand the words, they recognized them. In a way it was their song.

"Shan?"

"Uh-huh?"

She waited for a break in the song before she spoke again. "Do you think we'll be this close five years from now?"

He stared at her. "Why five years?"

"I don't know where it came from. It's a crazy thing to say, isn't it?" she asked.

"Maybe. Maybe it isn't, Donna."

"We've still got a long way to go. Don't we?"

He grinned. "We're both young, if that's what you mean."

"And, being young, we don't know how we'll feel five years from now. Right?"

He wiped his lips with the back of his big hand and looked at the sugar from the zeppole on his knuckles. Then he said, "Who knows how we'll feel six months from now."

"Then it is a crazy question."

He shrugged. His eyes had become dark and troubled.

"It is," she said softly. There was a tremor in her voice.

He turned to her, studied her, and slowly began to smile. "Not at all."

He leaned over and kissed her. They sat that way until the song was done and the singer had become silent.

Shan got up, softly humming the melody. "Let's go over to Mulberry Street and see the commedia."

"Will it be on?"

"They do it every year. They're great."

She hesitated. She wanted to sit with him and keep the moment alive. To sit and let him kiss her some more. And then she would speak to him.

"Come on. Don't you remember how you laughed? The routines are great. They're centuries old. The

characters—you gotta laugh just to look at them—
Pantalone. Arlecchino."

"I remember," she said gently. She remembered how
last year after seeing the show they had both read up
on the commedia dell'arte. Its history went back to the
Renaissance, just as this fair did.

"How about the *dottore* bit?" He pronounced the
word like an old Italian, thinning his voice and stretch-
ing the word out and relishing it. It pleased her to see
him acting this way. "It's an old W. C. Fields routine. I
mean, Fields got it from them. Lots of our comedy
comes from the old dell' arte companies."

"Yes. That's so," she said.

It warmed her to feel his sudden zest for life and to
see his eyes so bright with hope and feeling, and yet she
knew that really he was falling apart, and so her heart
was aching for him, feeling his agony.

"Yes. That's so," she said again, not realizing that
she was repeating herself.

"So, Donna?"

"Let's stay here just a little longer."

"Why?"

"There's something I want to talk to you about."

He waved his hand. "You did already. And I said,
who knows? *Quien sabe?*" He felt light and ebullient.

"Not that, Shan."

"Then what?"

She looked up at his glowing face and shook her
head. "It's nothing, Shan. Really nothing."

"Changing your mind?"

"Yes."

"Like a woman."

"You mean like a man."

He chuckled. "Then come on."

She linked her arm in his. "Okay. Let's go to the *dottore*." And as she said it, she tried to make her voice high and spirited, but she really wanted to say to him, Shan, let's go to the doctor. Not the *dottore* of past centuries but the doctor of today. To the psychiatrist. The doctor who heals sick minds. Please, Shan. For your sake. For mine. Before it's too late.

He pressed her hand as they hurried along. "There are times when I don't understand you," he said.

"Isn't that a fact!"

"Sure is."

"It's the secret of my charm."

"I guess it is."

Shan and Donna laughed, and the swirl of gaiety and high voices enveloped them. They walked past the garishly lit stands on their way to the platform stage on Mulberry Street where snatches of the traditional commedia dell' arte were put on. She thought again of the words his mother had spoken to her that morning, and saw again the suffering in Margaret Rourke's face.

We've got to help him, Donna. You and I.

What do you want me to do?

You must speak to him about going to a psychiatrist. You must, Donna. He won't listen to me. But I'm sure he'll listen to you. Isn't that so, Donna?

"Donna?"

The voice echoed the voice of her memory.

"Yes, Shan?"

"What's the matter? Your face got so sad."

"Did it, Shan?"

He nodded. "What's wrong, Donna?"

She was about to tell him, but now they were in the crowd massed in front of the outdoor stage. The play had begun. The characters were flouncing about the platform in their gaily colored costumes and characteristic masks, and the farce was in full swing, the audience was roaring with laughter.

"They're great, aren't they, Donna?"

"Yes."

"You were going to tell me what was wrong?" he asked.

But the action on the stage again drew their attention.

"I'll tell you later," Donna said, laughing despite herself.

"Is it important?" he asked, his eyes smiling.

"No, Shan."

There was a loud burst of laughter from the audience.

"Let's try to get closer to the stage," he said.

"Think we can?"

"Sure. If we use a little technique."

"Which is?"

"Just say, *Scusati, Signore e Signorina.* They'll let you through."

"Are you sure those are the right words?"

He shrugged. "They sound right. Come on, let's try it."

Bit by bit they made their way closer and closer to the platform, until they were near the little flight of steps that led up onto the stage. Just as they got to it, happy with themselves, and ready for a half-hour of pure enjoyment, the night fell apart.

It was then that illusion and reality jarred together and became one.

In the little kitchen on stage, three characters were sitting at the table, about to eat their supper. With a great characteristic flourish, Il Capitano grandly asked for the salt. Arlecchino answered with an exquisite and florid gesture of his own, ready to comply. Pantalone winked broadly at the audience and directed their attention to Arlecchino, for he, Pantalone, knew what was about to happen to Il Capitano. Arlecchino, mischievous as ever, instead of passing the tiny saltshaker, surreptitiously picked up a huge container on the floor at his side, the word "pepper" marked in large letters for all to see. Then he deftly spurted a flow of pepper right into the face of . . . Pantalone!

It was all done so artfully and yet so farcically that Shan and Donna laughed until the tears came. It was at that moment, at the height of the laughter that swelled about them, at that very moment Il Dottore came on stage, tall and lean, with the mask well over his narrow face and his large eyes peering through the two holes in the mask.

Like two dead eyes.

Suddenly Shan stopped laughing, his face paled, and he trembled. "No," he whispered.

The Dotorre bent over Pantalone and examined his eyes and then took out a huge, varicolored handkerchief and twirled it and twirled it until it waved like a silken flag. He bent solicitously over Pantalone and covered his face with the flag.

"Il Morte," Arlecchino wept.

The crowd roared with laughter.

"Shan?" Donna had turned to him.

"He's there," he said.

Shan's face had become taut. Beads of sweat were on his forehead. His lips were tight and thin.

"Shan," she said again.

"Don't you see him?" He kept pointing to the stage, to the tall, lean figure.

"Who, Shan?" She began to tremble with fear.

"Dammit, Donna, stop playing with me," he said harshly.

"I'm not."

He made a step toward the stage and turned again to her. His eyes were staring straight ahead of him, as if he didn't see her. His body was rigid. "The Dottore," he said in a hoarse whisper.

"What about him?" she pleaded.

Now he focused his eyes on her, and his face became savage and grim. "Can't you see? Are you blind?" He gripped her arm.

"Shan!"

"It's Lambert."

"You're hurting me."

But he didn't let go. "Don't you see what he's doing? Following me around wherever I go? Trying to drive me out of my skull?"

She pulled away from him. "Shan," she pleaded. "Let's get away from here. Please." She clung to him. "Please listen to me."

"No." He pushed her from him and rushed up the steps of the stage, and as he did a great silence came over the crowd.

The actors stopped and gaped at him. Pantalone and Arlecchino each froze in a different attitude of astonishment.

But the Dottore stood tall, straight, and rigid. The eyes peering through the holes of the mask. Cold and dead.

"Lambert!" Shan cried out. He went over and stood before him. "Take off your mask!" he shouted. "Or I'll rip it off!"

The man's eyes seemed to flicker. Then he slowly removed the mask.

"No," Shan whispered.

It was not Paul Lambert. Only an actor playing a role. Shan heard a fierce murmur rise from the crowd and begin to swell into a roar. In its midst, Donna's voice called frantically to him, "Shan!"

He looked past her and saw two policemen making their way through the crowd to the stage.

XIX

He walked down the steps of the precinct building, his mother and Donna on either side of him. They got into a cab and rode in silence all the way to Donna's apartment. As she got out, she smiled at him, her face pale and wan. "I'll call you tomorrow, Shan."

"Sure, Donna," he said.

She pressed his hand, but he didn't respond. He didn't even turn to watch her go into the building, but looked straight ahead. The cab went on.

"Shan?"

"Well?"

"We'll work this out together."

He didn't speak.

"Just don't get despondent."

"I'm not," he said.

But he felt despair and shame—shame at the way it all had turned out. The way Donna had to fight and plead for him. First with the sergeant, who wanted to book him immediately. He could've caused a riot there, Miss. Don't you see that? Then with the captain of the precinct. She even made them let her see the captain, while Shan stood there, silent, so very silent and looking so indifferent to it all, though inside he felt turmoil and darkness. Finally Donna was able to get them to send for Mrs. Rourke. And things took a turn for the better.

Then, Shan thought bitterly, everybody became so damned sympathetic and understanding about it all. He had a traumatic experience as a child and now there were some problems. But we're going to see about straightening them out, Captain. My son is going to get help. There will be no further difficulties with him. I can assure you of that. My husband was a dear friend of Justice Charles Connally. And I am still his friend. There'll be no more difficulties with Shan. No more.

Of course, Mrs. Rourke. I understand.

"You understand, don't you, Mother," Shan said aloud.

"What?"

"You always do." And he refused to say any more.

Later that night as he lay in bed, restless and sleepless, he heard a sound against the window that overlooked the garden.

Then he heard it again. It was a pelting sound, like that of a handful of gravel striking the window. Shan sat up in bed and then slowly got out of it. He went to the window and looked out and down.

An icy tremor went through him. He gasped.

There in the shadow of the garden, standing near the stone bench, was the Dottore, tall and silent, his mask over his lean face. And even from where Shan stood, he could see the two eyes staring through the two holes of the mask. Cold and glittering.

With a grating sound, Shan lifted the window high. "Lambert!" he cried out, his voice echoing against the night. "It's you this time. Dammit, it is you."

The Dottore bowed his head, a low bow, and as he did his hands went to the mask and slowly, ever so slowly, took it off. He straightened to his full height.

Now the shadows were on the man's face, the shadows and glints of moonlight. The large eyes glittered sardonically, relishing and savoring the moment. This time it was the face and being of Paul Lambert.

"Shan," he called up softly.

Shan stood by the window, rigid, cold, and unable to move.

"Come down, murderer."

Shan trembled violently.

"Come down. Let us talk."

Shan tried to speak, but the words wouldn't come.

"Let us talk of fires and murders. Do come down."

The voice taunted him softly, ever so softly.

"Shan." This time the voice came from behind him. He turned away sharply and saw his mother standing in the dark hallway, looking with pity and terror at him. "What is wrong?" she asked. "What, Shan?"

Without a word, he rushed to her and grabbed her arm and pulled her into the room and over to the window. "Look!" he shouted.

She stood there by him, shivering.

"Look!"

But there was no one in the garden. Nothing but the silence, the shadows, the moonlight glinting on the stone bench. The Dottore was gone.

"He was there. I saw him."

"Who, Shan?"

"I heard him. I tell you, I heard his voice."

"Shan, for God's sake . . ." She stopped.

They stood staring at each other. He could hear her words crying out at him, I can't take any more of this. I can't, Shan. They were there in her eyes, in her face.

Shan went over to the bed and sat down heavily. Suddenly he began to sob. It was a low, broken sound. As he wept, he heard from far down the street the high-pitched laughter of a man.

Soon the laughter died away, and Shan was quiet again. His mother stood in a corner of the shadowy room, white-faced and silent. Like a ghost.

XX

Just before morning, just before the pale sun started to rise, he had decided that he was going to kill Paul Lambert. There is no other way, he said to himself. If I don't kill him, he'll kill me.

He lay for hours in bed, his eyes staring up at the ceiling, watching the slow play of sunlight on it; then he got out of bed and went into the hallway and into the next room. He opened the door of the closet and stood a long time, searching through the diving gear that was stored there. After a while, he picked up the spear gun and hefted it. Thoughtfully, coldly, he considered its merits and disadvantages. He smiled to himself, and took the gun and went back to his room and over to the window that overlooked the garden. He took aim at the stone bench and pretended that he was firing a spear into the head of a man sitting there. The back of the head, just at the nape of the neck. He watched the downward flight of the spear, saw the spurt of blood. He shuddered, and then the image vanished. Shan lifted the gun from his shoulder and stood as if he were concentrating on a math problem.

Finally he decided against that method. There was too much chance of missing or just wounding the man on the bench. The man must be killed. The job must be done cleanly and effectively. There must be no foul-up. None. He placed the gun back in its corner of the closet and closed the door.

I have to get nearer to him when I do it, Shan thought. Maybe I can set him up another way.

He went back to his room and over to the bureau. He opened the bottom drawer and there, under some sweaters, he found the Pawkii, a Finnish hunting knife that he had bought a year ago. He had been walking along Flatbush Avenue and had seen the knife in the window of a sporting-goods store. He didn't know why he had bought it at the time. He had no need for it. But now he knew. Everything is fated in life, he said to himself. Everything. So what the hell's the use?

The Pawkii had a long, narrow blade that was as sharp as a needle's point. He took the knife out of its sheath and held it up to the thin rays of the sun. The blade gleamed triumphantly.

"Yes," he whispered.

He felt a warm thrill coursing through him. His face became hot and flushed, his eyes large and dancing. A wide smile was on his lips. Once he had drunk too much wine at a Christmas party, and now, as he stood looking at the knife, he was experiencing the same feeling. It was a very heady sensation. And at the same time, somewhere in his being, he felt repelled and nauseous.

Shan brandished the knife and made some savage thrusts with it. Yes, this should do it, he said to himself.

"It should," he said aloud, and the sound of his voice pleased and exhilarated him. He felt like laughing out loud. Just laughing and letting himself go. Ah, it was such a good feeling to know that he was finally about to free himself, once and for all. I'll get that crazy bastard off my back forever.

Yet while he was saying that, a chilling dread went through him, and he asked himself, Am I as crazy as he is? Am I?

"Mother," he said aloud. It was almost like a cry for help.

He shook his head grimly. I've got to do it. Or he'll kill me first. That's where it's at. I'm caught in a box, and the only way out is to slash my way. That's the only course left to me.

Crazy? No, dammit, logical. Survival, man. Survival.

He put the knife into its sheath and the sheath on his desk. Then he sat there a long time, thinking about how to set Lambert up for the kill.

"Shan?" It was his mother's voice, soft and tentative, from the foot of the stairs.

"Yes?" He got up and went to the threshold of the room.

"Are you up?" she asked.

"That's right." He wanted to laugh and call down to her, Of course I'm up. How would I answer you if I wasn't? What kind of a question is that anyway? He began to chuckle.

"Would you like to have breakfast?"

He stood against the doorjamb, tall, with the sunlight striking sharply on his blond hair and fair face. There was a sparkle in his dark blue eyes. If Donna were standing on the stairs and looking up she would say again, But he's a Viking. And then she would see the anguish, the mad anguish, hidden behind the sparkle, and be silent.

"Breakfast? Anything you say, Mother." He felt lighthearted and gay.

"Some scrambled eggs?"

"You're the cook, old girl."

There was a pause, and then he heard "You'll be down soon?" Her voice had become tentative again.

"Call me when you're ready," he said.

"All right, Shan."

He went back to his desk, chuckling softly to himself. He sat down again and took out a sheet of paper and made doodles on it, while he thought more of his plan. Soon he drew a diagram of his street and his house and then a car parked alongside of it, and then he drew in the lamppost and filled in the dark sky. Never once did he think of what would happen to him after the murder. His whole concentration was on one thing: how to kill Paul Lambert. Just that and no more.

Soon he heard her call up, "It's ready, Shan."

He realized with a shock that time had raced by. It seemed only seconds ago that he was speaking to her. "Okay." He folded the paper carefully and put it into the back pocket of his jeans and went down the stairs and into the kitchen.

She smiled at him. "There's a glow in your face, Shan."

"I feel pretty good," he said.

"I'm glad," she murmured.

They ate silently.

"Shan?"

He gazed across the table at her. The fearful, tentative look had come back into her eyes. For some reason he thought of a barefoot girl carefully picking her way among sharp, gleaming shards of glass.

Then he remembered that he had once gone swimming with Donna at a country lake and there were a lot of hard, sharp-edged stones just at the edge of the water. He had wanted to carry her, but she insisted on walking, and she—

"Well?" he asked, breaking off the image of Donna.

His mother picked up a paper napkin that lay near her plate and folded it carefully with her small, delicate fingers. Then she spoke. "I . . . I made an appointment with Dr. Loeb."

He felt the back of his neck prickle, and for an instant he felt a chill of fear.

"Who's he?" Shan asked.

"A . . . a psychiatrist."

"Oh," he said softly.

It was exactly as he figured.

"He's a very good one, Shan."

"I'm sure he is."

She unfolded the napkin and sat for a while looking at it. "You're not angry at me? Are you?"

He smiled at her. The fear had gone from him. He felt strangely calm and uncaring.

"What else could you do?" he said. "The way I've been acting."

"Yes," she murmured. He could barely hear her voice.

"I don't mind seeing a shrink," he said, but inside he felt, So what? I know what I have to do. So what's the difference what the shrink says?

"The doctor is a very busy man. But he'll see us for a few minutes today."

"Us?"

"Well, I . . . I thought I'd go along with you."

"Be my guest."

She paled but didn't speak.

"What time?" he asked.

"One thirty."

"I'll be there."

"Thanks, Shan."

"It's I who should thank you, Mother." Then he burst out laughing.

"Shan . . ." She looked at him and then got up and went out of the kitchen. He knew that she had begun to cry.

He rose from his chair and took a few steps in her direction. His heart was sore and aching for her. He wanted to put his arms about her and comfort her. And at the same time to break down and weep and say, Help me, please, please help me.

Mother, dear Mother.

"Mother," he whispered.

But he went no more than the few steps and he came to a standstill. What the hell's the use, he found himself thinking.

Shan went slowly back to his chair and sat down. He took the paper from his back pocket and spread it out on the table and began to study it. Soon he forgot about her. Completely.

XXI

He sat talking to Dr. Loeb. The Pawkii lay secure on his belt, under his jacket. He was starting to get used to its being there, as if he had been carrying a deadly knife for many years. It was becoming an essential part of him.

"We're here to get acquainted with each other. All right, Shannon? Or shall I call you . . .?" He paused and waited for Shan to speak.

"Shan."

The doctor nodded and smiled. "Then it's Shan."

He was a small, compact man with a bald head and clear brown eyes that seemed to smile. His voice was quiet and even. It was pleasant to listen to him. "I hope we'll get to be friends. To get to know each other. How does that sound to you?"

"Okay with me."

"Good."

They were alone in the office; his mother waited in the reception room. Shan sat in an easy chair, his long legs spread out in front of him, lounging. The doctor sat behind his desk. The afternoon sun came into the room and hovered over them. It was all so quiet and sunny and pleasant. Like an oasis. Shan felt calm and at ease, yet the undercurrent of anxiety, of bitterness and of terror, never really left him.

"We all have problems, Shan. Don't you agree?"

"Yes."

"We're human. All of us."

"I guess so."

The doctor shook his head gently. "No guessing about it. We all are subject to the human condition. As far as I know, no one has yet been able to escape that fact. We love, we fear, we do stupid things. We do brilliant things. We cry, we suffer, and we even kill. Isn't that so?"

"Yes," Shan said.

"Shan, as you know, I spoke to your mother before you came in here. I wanted to get from her a perspective. Her perspective. Some facts, some background, and some opinion." He spread his hands out and smiled. "No secrets. What I discussed with her you will find out. Could you tell me how your father died?"

"My father?" The question startled Shan. He had not expected it.

"Try to think, Shan. Try to go back in memory."

"I . . . I really don't know," Shan said.

"You have no remembrance? Not even a vague one?"

"Nothing," Shan said.

The doctor's fingers thrummed gently on the desk. "Can I tell you what your mother says?"

"Okay."

"That he had a heart attack. Well, Shan?"

"I . . . I think it was that way."

"You think so?"

"Yes."

"It was a very hot day. Can you remember what he was doing on that hot day?"

Shan shook his head. "No."

"Was he out walking? Riding a bicycle? Driving a car?"

"I . . . I don't remember."

"Well, shall I tell you what your mother says happened?"

"Okay."

"He was out riding a bicycle. He collapsed. I understand that he was a young man."

Shan was silent.

"You also were young, Shan. Do you believe that you were old enough to know what had happened?"

"I guess I was," Shan said.

"And to remember? How do you feel about that?"

Shan shrugged. "Maybe I should remember."

"But you don't," the man said softly. And Shan thought, almost in panic, This fellow's too sharp for me. I'd better watch myself or he'll find out what I'm planning to do to Lambert. And I don't want that. Nothing's going to stop me from killing that bastard. Not after all the suffering and agony he's put me through.

The doctor was speaking again. "How do you feel about your father, Shan?"

"What?"

"Do you miss him very much?"

"Yes."

"Would you care to tell me a little about him? What kind of a man he was?"

Shan shrugged and finally spoke. "He was good to me. I felt that I could go to him and sort of . . . well, get some comfort from him. He was a big man, and he wasn't afraid of anybody. And when I'd have one of my nightmares and think the house was burning up, he was the first to come into the room and pick me up in his arms. Yes, he was a big and powerful man, and maybe if he was around now . . ." Shan stopped, his voice whispering away.

"Go on," the doctor said softly, persuasively, but Shan didn't even hear him.

"He was a big man," Shan murmured. "And yet something seemed to be eating him up . . . I guess I have a good idea now what it was."

"What?"

Shan shook his head and was silent.

"How about your mother?"

"I love her. But I guess I don't really trust her anymore."

"Would you care to tell me why?"

Shan shook his head. "Let's just leave it as it is."

"Do you resent my asking these questions?"

"You're paid for it, aren't you?"

The doctor smiled broadly. "I am, Shan. Quite well."

They were silent. The doctor leaned forward and looked appraisingly at Shan. For an instant Shan was certain he knew about the knife and his plan to kill

Lambert. He almost expected to hear the man speak out and ask for the knife.

Give me the knife, Shan, or I'll have to call the police.

"Would you care to talk about the birthday card?" the doctor asked.

"What about it?"

"Would you like to tell me about it?"

Shan grinned. "I wrote it, Dr. Loeb. I wrote it and then put it there on the bureau, while nobody was around to see. *Happy Birthday, Murderer.* That's what I wrote on the card. Do you want to know why? Because I am a birthday murderer. Isn't that so, Doctor? Isn't that what my mother told you? Isn't it? You say there are no secrets between us. Didn't she tell you that?" A mad glint had come into Shan's eyes. He felt light and sardonic and yet, strangely, almost on the point of tears.

God, why did I even let myself be brought here? Why? I'm close to the breaking point. I can tell that now. This bastard will lead me on and I'll be trapped. Then they'll take the knife away from me. I should get up and walk out of the office.

But then again Shan wanted to stay and see how it all turned out. He felt that he was like a spectator at a murder drama. Will the murderer be caught? Will the crime be prevented? What will happen?

He heard the doctor speak again.

"Let's say just for the sake of discussion that you are a murderer. Do you think you should be punished for your deed?"

"No," Shan said. And it surprised him how easily and sincerely he had said it.

"Ah," the doctor murmured.

"I was a kid. I didn't know what I was doing." Shan's voice rose. "I've punished myself a thousand times in a thousand different ways. Isn't that enough? They talk of heaven and hell being outside this life. The hereafter. You have to die to get there. But that isn't so. It isn't. I've been in hell all the time, even when I was laughing and happy. Even then I was suffering inside me. All those years. I've been paying and paying. Why? Why? For what?"

And then he said something that startled him, for he didn't know where it came from. "Maybe I never even did it. How the hell do I know?" He stopped and then said in a low, puzzled voice, "That was a crazy thing to say."

"Why do you think it was crazy, Shan?"

"Because I did kill him."

"How do you know?"

"Christ, everybody knows I did it. Didn't my mother tell you? I set fire to him. I burned him up."

"Can you remember doing it?"

"No. No. Nothing. But last night in a nightmare I saw George Lambert. He pleaded with me not to do it. Not to light the match." Shan's voice broke. "But I didn't listen to him."

The doctor sat there looking at him. Shan suddenly rose from his chair. "Let me alone. I don't want to go into this anymore."

"Just a few more minutes," the doctor said very gently after a pause. "I believe we're getting into something very important to you, Shan."

"Let's cut it off," Shan said. He went to the door.

The doctor rose and came from behind the desk. "I want to tell you something. Please stay and listen."

Shan waited, his hand on the doorknob.

"I don't believe you wrote that card."

Shan trembled and stared at the man.

"How do you know?"

Dr. Loeb shook his head. "I don't. It's just a feeling. An intuition. You get that after many years of practice, of seeing patients."

"Then who did write the card?" Shan asked.

The doctor stood and thought deeply, and then he said, "I'm afraid I can't answer that."

"If I didn't write it, someone had to do it."

"You're asking me the same question again, Shan."

"It's like going around in circles. Isn't it?"

"Yes."

Shan wanted to burst out, Now do you see what I've been living through? Do you see? All of you, damn you? No, no one really sees. No one. "No one," he murmured out loud.

The doctor put his arm tenderly about Shan. "Why don't you sit down again and let's talk some more. And perhaps we'll find out some more?"

"No," Shan said and moved away from the doctor. "I've had enough for a while."

"All right then. Could you come here the day after tomorrow?"

"Wednesday?"

"Yes. In the evening. I'm making time for you because I feel an urgency. I do want to help you."

"I'll be here."

"I want you to promise me one thing."

"Yes?"

"That if you feel any need for me before that time, you'll call me." The man's eyes looked steadily into Shan's.

"I promise," Shan said. But to himself he said, I'll never keep that promise. Because tonight I'm killing Lambert, and after that I surely won't be seeing you. You probe too deeply, dear doctor. You're the last person in the world I'll want to see after tonight. The very last one.

"Good-bye, Shan."

"Good-bye, Dr. Loeb."

Shan closed the door, shutting out the view of the doctor.

XXII

"Shan."

He didn't answer.

"Shan," his mother said again. They were sitting in a cab on their way back to the house. He turned to her, a veiled, absent look in his eyes. "Yes?"

"I . . . I just wanted to know how things turned out."

"With the shrink?"

"Yes."

The agonized feelings and words he had said in the office came back to him, but he kept control of himself, and he said with a smile, "Fine."

"You like him?"

He nodded. "Yes. I think he's pretty competent."

If I'm going to do it right, I've got to keep them all

away from me, he said to himself. Build a ring about me and keep them out. Never let them know what I'm really thinking and feeling. I let the doctor come too close. I can't make the same mistake with her.

"I'm glad," she said, and her voice trembled with emotion.

"I have faith in him," Shan said. "Is he a Freudian?"

"I really don't know, Shan."

He didn't speak for a while, as he thought out what next to say. "Well," he finally said to her, "I asked because he seems interested in the Oedipus complex. And I understand that Freudians go in for that a lot."

"Oh."

"You know, the jealousy bit between son and father over mother. We discussed it in school when we studied *Hamlet.*" He paused as the thought and image of Donna came to him. Of Donna sitting in class with him, his eyes glancing across the room to her soft profile, the warm feeling spreading through him, and suddenly he wanted to shout to the driver to stop the cab and let him out. He wanted to run, just to run away from his mother, away from Dr. Loeb, away from Paul Lambert, away, away, until he found Donna and . . . and as he was feeling all this, he heard another part of himself speaking to his mother. "Dr. Loeb and I talked about it." A part that seemed cut off from him. Easy and controlled. "He pointed out that the son's jealousy can extend to anybody who takes an interest in the mother. He made me understand things."

"I'm so glad."

"I believe he's going to help me a lot."

"As long as you feel he's going to help you, Shan." She squeezed his hand.

"Mother," he said.

She turned to him.

"When are you seeing Lambert again?"

He knew that she was seeing him that night; he had heard her speak to Paul Lambert on the phone that very morning. Shan had listened from outside the room.

"Paul?" She had paled.

"Uh-huh."

"Why, Shan?"

He smiled at her. To himself he said, Just keep it smooth. You're doing fine. Very fine. But the other part of him almost shrieked, Damn fool, watch yourself. She'll get wise and you'll blow it all. Be careful. This is crucial. You've got to set it up right or the plan will fall apart.

"No reason to get upset. Just tell me."

"I . . . well, tonight."

Now watch yourself. Do it right, Shan.

"Is he coming to the house?"

That's vital. The heart of the plan.

She shook her head. "I . . . we thought it better that he didn't."

"You were going to meet him downtown?"

"Yes. We planned to go to the theater. But it's tentative."

All right. Now be careful. Do it easy. You've got it made.

"You mean it all depended on how I felt?" he said.

"Yes, Shan. That was understood."

"Well, you can see how encouraged I am."

"I do, Shan."

"So go and have a good time."

The cab turned down their block. The day was warm and gray. Along the sides of the street the plane trees stood, tall and motionless.

"But why did you ask me about Paul?"

A wave of fear swept over him. She suspects something is wrong. But then he said to himself, You damned idiot, keep her away. Keep them all away. Think. Think and you'll be in the clear again.

"Isn't it interesting, Mother, that you call him Paul and I no longer do that?"

She didn't speak.

"That's one of the problems I took up with the doctor."

That's better. Much better. You're back on the track again. Just stay with the doctor. She believes in him. Stay with him.

"And?"

"He feels that I am much too jealous of Paul. You see, I can call him Paul, too. The doctor seems to be working his magic on me."

"Jealous?"

"Well, it's complex. That's one of the words the doctor used. 'Complex.' The reason I asked about Lambert was that Dr. Loeb wants me to have a talk with him."

"With Paul?"

"Yes. He feels it would do the two of us a lot of good."

"It would, Shan. It certainly would."

"Then you agree, too?"

"Of course, Shan. What a question."

He felt relief. Then she doesn't suspect. I've kept her

off and now it's all set up. That bastard will be here tonight after the theater. Good. Very good. His hand went to the knife on his belt, just to make sure that it was still there. Then it closed tightly about the handle.

"Good," he whispered, but she did not hear him.

The cab stopped in front of their house. Mrs. Rourke opened her purse, took out the money, and gave it to Shan to pay the driver. Then they got out and walked to the door.

"That would be wonderful, Shan."

"Yes. Dr. Loeb has great faith in the idea. He wants the two of us to sit quietly and talk things out."

Her eyes glowed. "It's just what Paul has always wanted."

"Is it, Mother?" A touch of bitterness and hatred came into his voice. He couldn't hold it back, and now he looked at her with dread. Dammit, why did I open my mouth? All was clear and won.

But she was too enthused to notice. "Yes. Yes. He does want to get close to you. He does, Shan. You must try to believe that."

He smiled gently at her. "I'm trying to, Mother."

"That's all you have to do," she said, her voice almost breaking. "Believe, Shan. Just believe."

He put his arm about her. "I will. Now you have a good time tonight. I'll call him tomorrow and see about our getting together. But don't say anything. I want to surprise Paul."

She reached up to him and drew his head down to her and kissed him. "Shan," she said. "I'm so glad."

They went into the house together.

XXIII

He had watched many times how the police broke into locked cars when they wanted to tow them away. Now he used the same technique. He forced the wire into the crack between the small glass panel and the rest of the window and slid it down till he hooked the inner handle, and then he pulled sharply and yanked the door open. It was as simple as that.

He stood for a moment glancing warily about. The block was bleak, silent and empty. Then he looked up at the house and saw the light shining in the living room. Lambert was still there with his mother, but he would soon be coming out. It was already a quarter past one.

Shan opened the back door of the car and sat down inside, waiting for Paul Lambert to appear. As he waited in the darkness, he went over the plan again. It now had the clarity and precision of a completed circle. Before he had been concerned only with how to kill Lambert. Now he had figured out how he could kill him and get away with it.

Complete the circle, one of his high-school math teachers had said. Always complete the circle. Shan smiled as he thought of the small, gray-haired man standing before the class, speaking with such warmth and pleasantness. The man had been so mild and so peaceful, so far, far away from violence. It had been one of Shan's favorite classes. He always looked forward to it.

There would be no suspicions. None whatsoever. He would take Lambert's watch and wallet, and anything else of value that could be removed easily. Then he would get rid of them where they would never be found again. He knew a bridge in the park, where the water below was deep; he would drop the watch and wallet into the night-black water and let them sink till they lay on the bottom of the lake, hidden away forever. The police would be certain that the man had been killed by a mugger.

I'll be rid of him forever, Shan thought. And once I'm rid of him, this torture will stop and I'll be sound and healthy again. It's like ridding yourself of a cancer. You cut it out, once and for all. Then, slowly but surely, the body recovers and forgets, for ever and ever.

He grinned to himself in his little corner of darkness. Then he heard the front door of the house open and close. It was a muffled sound. Shan took the knife out of the sheath and held it tightly in his damp hand. Then he slid off the seat and huddled low in the black well of the car.

He waited, his mouth shut in a thin line, his breath coming through his flared nostrils. His heart pounded, louder and louder, until he began to dread that Lambert might hear it.

The front door of the car opened and then there was the sound of a body getting in and sitting down. The back of the seat trembled under the impact of the body; then there was the sharp, metallic crack of the door being shut. The motor started up and the car began to move forward.

Shan lifted himself to the back of the seat and with a silent thrust put the needle point of the blade to Lambert's neck. "Just keep moving," he said.

The man didn't say a word. There was a slight tremor and that was all. His hands tightened just a bit about the steering wheel. He kept looking straight ahead of him.

"Turn at the corner. Then go down the block to the end."

Shan was astonished at the man's iron composure. It made him hate him all the more. If only Lambert would cry out and plead for mercy. If he would only do that. But Lambert drove as if he were alone in the car.

"Right there. Under the tree," Shan said.

The car stopped. Ahead of them stretched the empty expanse of the park. The lights of the walks were distant and cold against the night. A soft wind made the branches of the trees tremble. The leaves shook, like soundless, ghostly bells.

"So now you are about to kill me," Lambert said harshly.

"Yes."

"Then do it."

Confronted with the act, the final act, Shan hesitated.

"Just a little pressure. That's all there is to it," Lambert said. "Press and it's all over."

Just say a little more and I'll do it, Shan thought grimly. Just keep on with your smooth talk. Keep on!

"You've planned it well, Shan. With a murderer's brain."

The wind shook the branches of the trees again. The leaves began to toll again, like soundless death knells. A great sweat had broken out all over Shan.

"Do it."

"Yes!"

He was about to plunge the knife into the man's neck when suddenly he heard himself cry out, "Why don't you let me alone! I want to live. That's all I want. Why don't you let me? Why?"

There was a pause. "Because no one ever forgets a murder, Shan," Lambert said in a flat and even voice. "Neither the murderer nor the victim. And I am the victim. The true victim. My son has long found his peace. I have none."

Shan saw the lights in the park begin to blink and waver, and he knew that tears had come to his eyes. Yet he still held the point of the blade to the man's neck.

"None," Lambert said again in a savage whisper. "Look what you've done to my life and what you're still doing. Murderer. If it weren't for you, I could love your mother. Love her and live happily ever after. But I think of you all the time. Even when I'm holding her in my arms. Even then you continue to kill." His voice rose. "Murderer. You destroy everything. With one match you set fire to my life. Nothing is left for me. Nothing. And you ask me to let you live?"

His voice died away. And suddenly Shan realized that the two had finally become equal. Yes, we're equal, he said to himself. We're caught in the same hatred. In the same sickness. In the same fate. And there's nothing either of us can do about it. My death will free you. Only that will do it. I can see it all so clearly now. And I? If I don't kill you now, I'm doomed. It's as simple as that.

Shan's hand tightened about the knife until his knuckles gleamed whitely.

"You'd better kill me, Shan. For as God is my witness, I'm going to kill you." The man sat there rigid as a statue, waiting for his death. "Do it, you fool! Or I will kill you. If you don't have what it takes now, you never will! Then I can take my time, make you suffer even more. No one will believe you!"

Shan trembled violently and then slowly drew the knife away. He got out of the car and slammed the door shut. The car went off, and he watched it till it was lost in the night. Then he sat down heavily on the curb.

"Fool!"

The knife dropped from his hand and clattered to the concrete. I couldn't cross over the line, Shan said to himself. I just couldn't. Now what can I do to save myself?

"Dammed fool," he said aloud.

The night wind rustled the leaves of the tree, and this time he thought he could hear the tiny, soundless bells . . . then all was still again. After a while, he got up and went home. But he lay awake all night, feeling isolated and terrified.

XXIV

I couldn't cross over the line and so now I must die. In the morning, he sat on the stone bench in the garden, waiting for his death. He knew now that it was inevitable—and very soon. Up to now Lambert had played with him as a cat with a mouse, but the game had become much too dangerous for him. He had almost died himself. It will come soon, Shan said to himself. This afternoon. Or tonight. But it will come.

The sun filtered through the branches to his lonely figure. His blond hair was burnished; his face glowed with a pale light.

"Shan?"

He looked up and saw his mother standing before him.

"Yes?"

"Paul just called."

Shan trembled slightly, ever so slightly. His mother noticed nothing.

"He asked me to meet him downtown. Do you mind if I go off?"

"Why should I mind?"

She shrugged. "I just didn't know if you wanted to be left alone in the house."

"I'm old enough to be left alone."

She sat down by him. "You seem rather quiet today."

"Am I?"

"Yes." Her eyes rested on him tenderly.

"Just thinking, Mother. That's all."

She put her hand on his. "You haven't had your talk with Paul."

He smiled thinly. "I will."

"Do you want to come along with me now?"

He shook his head.

"I'm sure Paul would be glad to have you. And you can talk."

"We have to do it alone, Mother. Just the two of us."

"I understand."

"Just Paul and I." He almost whispered the words.

"Yes."

She pressed his hand, he felt the warmth of her fingers, and for a moment he thought of Donna and felt a sharp yearning for her. I should call her.

"Then you'll be all right, Shan?"

I should call Dr. Loeb. I shouldn't die this way. Somewhere there should be a way out.

"Shan?"

He turned to her. "But there is no way out, is there, Mother?"

"What, Shan?" She was looking at him anxiously.

"Nothing. Nothing, Mother," and he smiled.

But the anxiety would not leave her.

"Why don't you come with us, Shan? Why sit around the house?"

"I'd rather stay here," he said, his voice hard.

They sat in silence, close to each other. The leaves of the huge old tree lay about them. He looked down at them and thought, They've fallen early this year, so very early. So much before their time. It's unfair. So unfair. He felt an aching pity for the fallen leaves.

"Mother," he said.

"Yes?"

"I've been thinking. You know, in a way, all my life I've felt much older than I really was."

"You always have been, Shan," she said gently.

"Ah," he whispered.

"You're some years ahead of yourself. Your father always said that."

"Did he?"

"Yes. He saw it very clearly."

"Young as I was."

She nodded.

"What do you think did it, Mother?"

"I . . . I don't know, Shan." She shrugged.

"I wish you'd tell me," he said.

She sighed. "Perhaps it was the tragedy that happened to you, Shan."

"The birthday party."

"Yes," she said in a low voice.

"Not only to me," he said. "It was a fire that seared all of us, wasn't it?"

She looked away from him, and he could see the outlines of her delicate profile against the rays of the sun. Suddenly he realized that with all her delicacy, her smallness, her readiness to tears, she was the strongest of all of them, the most endurable. She would survive his death, as she had survived his father's. It made him bitter and sad all at once.

"It's a fire that has never really stopped burning. Has it, Mother?"

"I don't know what you mean, Shan," she said, still not looking at him.

"In a way, it killed my father, didn't it, Mother?"

She turned sharply to him, a stricken look on her face. "What do you mean, Shan?"

"His heart attack," he said quietly.

"What about it?"

"Didn't it really come from his worry and sense of guilt over what had happened? He grieved over it till it finally got to him."

"No. No. You must never think that."

"He felt that he was more guilty than I was. After all, I was a child. He was my father. In some way he should have prevented the murder. Wasn't that it?"

"Shan, please. Never say that again." Her words, the anguish in her eyes, told him that he had groped and found the harsh truth.

"But it's so, isn't it?" he went on.

"Shan."

He shrugged and then sighed. "I won't say it anymore," he said gently.

"Or think it."

"All right. I won't think it anymore."

"Shan," she pleaded.

He reached his hand to her and touched her face, as he would a child's. He felt an ache within him for the pain and anguish he had just given her. And, in a way, had always given her. From the very first instant that he had lit the match. From the flare of the flame.

Mother, Mother, Mother, he said within.

"I'll discuss this with Dr. Loeb," he said aloud. "I'm sure he'll help me clear it up."

He saw her face light up, and that was what he wanted. Why not give her some hope? What the hell does it cost?

"You're seeing the doctor tomorrow night?"

"Yes."

"Just have faith in him, Shan. Please."

"I do have faith," he said.

She kissed his cheek. "It will all work out, Shan."

"It will."

Then she said, "Were you able to sleep last night?"

He gazed at her sadly. "Yes, very well," he lied.

XXV

It was six thirty, just as darkness was gliding in through the trees, when he heard the front doorbell ring. He went cautiously to it and looked through the frosted glass pane and saw the tall figure of a man. It was Lambert. But then, as Shan bent closer to the glass, he saw that he was mistaken. Shan opened the door on the chain.

"Shannon Rourke?"

Shan gazed at the face of the actor who had played Dottore. The eyes had a bright and almost scornful cast to them, just as when the man had taken off the mask and revealed to Shan that he was not Paul Lambert.

"Yes?"

"I have a letter for you," the man said in a low,

measured voice, as if he were still on stage playing his role. He handed it through the slight opening, bowed low, then turned and went away without another word.

Shan shut the door and locked it. He went into the living room, put on the lamp, and sat down to read the letter. It was written in his own handwriting.

Dear Mother,

I find that I cannot go on anymore. Each day is more difficult than the one that went before it. No matter how hard I try I can't forget that I am a murderer. No one can erase it from my mind. Not even Dr. Loeb. It is too much of a burden to carry with me all of my life. No one ever forgets a murder, not the murderer, not the victim.

I keep seeing the face of George Lambert before me. He refuses to forget what I did to him. Nor will he forgive.

Good-bye,
Shan

He was about to put the letter back into the envelope when he heard the phone ring. He sat there and let it ring, and then finally he got up and answered it.

"Hello?" His voice sounded strange and distant to him. As if it were another person who was speaking.

"Shan?" It was Donna.

"Yes. It's Shan," he said.

"I'm glad I got you in."

"Why?"

"Because I'd like to see you."

"Oh."

"I spoke to your mother yesterday afternoon."

"And?"

"She said you got on pretty well with the shrink. Is she right?"

"I guess so," he said.

"Then things are beginning to look up."

"Yes, Donna. They are. They really are." But within he ached with despair.

"You don't know how glad I am to hear that, Shan."

"I know you are, Donna," he said gently. And he wanted to break down and cry, wanted to say to her, Donna, I'm lost. Can't you see it? Can't you hear it in my voice? There's no way to go anymore. Donna, Donna. He's going to kill me tonight and that's the way it should be. Murderers should die. They should never be allowed to go on. They only bring misery to themselves and to everybody else. Isn't that so, Donna?

"Will we see each other tonight, Shan?"

"Tonight?" he echoed.

"Uh-huh."

"How about tomorrow night?"

"Shan, there's a Redford movie at the Rialto. One of his old ones we haven't seen."

"So we'll see it tomorrow night."

"But tonight is the last night. Something else is playing tomorrow.

"So we'll miss it."

"But we shouldn't, Shan. We really shouldn't."

He felt that somehow she sensed that she was fighting for his life, that if she could get him out of the house and with her, he would live.

"I'm not in the mood for it," he said.

"Then we could just walk around. Just be together."

It's no use, Donna. I made my choice last night. I didn't kill him. You don't get another chance in this life, Donna. You light a match and you blow it out. Then everything goes black on you. That's it, Donna.

You light a match
You light a match
You light a match
Why did I ever light that first match?
Don't you know?
Don't you?

"Then it's tomorrow night, Shan?" Now he heard her voice.

He didn't answer.

"I miss you," she said.

Still he didn't answer.

"I want you to hold me and kiss me."

He breathed as if in pain. "Tomorrow night," he said.

There was a slight pause.

"Good-bye, Shan."

He couldn't bring himself to say good-bye to her. Slowly he put the receiver back onto its hook. Then he sat there, the letter in his hand. The darkness was now in the house.

XXVI

He left the front door unlocked. Then,
slowly and deliberately, he climbed the stairs
to his room. He propped the envelope against
the clock on the bureau. Then he went across the room
to his bed and lay down on it, fully clothed. Let death
come now, he said to himself. Let it all be over.

He found himself thinking of George Lambert, and
soon he saw his young face before him, pleading with
Shan not to light the match.

"Leave me alone, George," Shan whispered. "I've
suffered enough already. You've had your revenge. Let
me rest. Please, George. Please."

The anguished young face shimmered into the darkness, and Shan let his breath out in relief and lay there

waiting. After a long, long time, an almost eternal time, he heard the front door open and close. Heard it as from a long, long distance. Then the sound of footsteps coming up the steps filled the emptiness of the house. A pause of vast silence. After that he heard the footsteps along the hallway, sounding with a hollow echoing, finally stopping just outside the room. Silence. A humming silence. He saw the figure filling the doorway. It was Paul Lambert.

"So you are here, just as your mother said." The voice was toneless, flat and low. The silence seemed to surround it. "I told her I'd have a little talk with you and then meet her later. Is that all right with you, Shan?"

Shan's lips were shut tight.

"You knew I'd come. Didn't you?"

"Yes," Shan breathed out in a low sigh.

"You didn't have to leave the front door unlocked, Shan." The figure still filled the doorway, its voice now soft and mocking. "I would've come in anyway. As I have in the past. Many times. At will. Even when you and your mother were in the house. Even then. I was here, like your very shadow. I know every nook and corner of this building. Top to bottom. What do you think of that?" A soft, almost toneless laugh, and then the voice continued on. "I even have a copy of the original architectural plans. I've studied it for years. I have keys to the front door, to the garden door, to the cellar door, to the downstairs apartment door. I have so many keys, Shan. So many." The toneless laughter again. "I've studied this house for years. As I've studied your death for years, down to its last detail."

Shan saw the glint in the figure's eyes and then the glint of the gun barrel with the silencer.

"The last detail."

Lambert came into the room and stood in its center.

"It all started with a birthday party. It all started with a fire. And so it should begin its end with a fire. Don't you think so, Shan?"

Shan heard the crackle of a match being lit.

"Isn't that poetic justice?"

He saw the flame of a candle flicker and sputter, and then the shadows and lights on Lambert's lean, haggard face.

"Just lie there, Shan. As he did," the voice rustled and whispered.

Against his will, Shan began to shake with fear and horror. Dear God, he said to himself, I don't want to die this way. Not this way.

"I'll let you burn as he did. But not enough to kill you." The eyes were now wild. "That will come later. First I want you to suffer, suffer the agonies that he did."

"Lambert, please." The words forced their way out of Shan's being.

"He must've said 'please,' too, didn't he? Did you listen to him? Did you?"

The figure approached the bed and the flame came closer and closer, and then it began to sear into Shan's flesh, and as it did, a voice within Shan cried out, *No. No. I want to live!*

"I didn't kill George!" he heard himself scream.

He didn't know where the thought came from. All he knew was that he had to say something. Anything to

throw Lambert off balance. Anything to hold him off.
Anything. I've got to save my life.

"He killed himself!" Shan screamed again as the
flame seared into his flesh once more. "He killed himself. *Himself!*"

The flame wavered and drew slightly away.

"Because you and your wife were going to separate.
He couldn't stand that. He couldn't."

"Liar!"

Shan sprang from the bed and faced the dark figure.
I am a liar. But I'm going to live. Damn you, I'm going
to find a way to live. I've suffered too much. Too many
years.

"Killed himself. It comes back to me." The words
poured out of him. "He started the fire, not I." They
came out of themselves, from deep in his being. "That's
the way it happened."

"Liar! Liar!"

Lambert struck with a wild fury at Shan, hitting him
hard on the jaw with the butt of the gun. Shan staggered
against the wall, dazed and bleeding. Yet he continued
to cry out to the man.

"He set fire to the bed. Then he told me to get out of
the room."

And while he was crying out, in those split seconds
of agony and terror, he knew he was telling the truth. It
did happen that way. Now, at last, he could see clearly
the scene in George Lambert's bedroom twelve years
before. They were all so sure that he, Shan, had caused
the fire—they were so horrified by the thought that
George had committed suicide—that they had even
convinced Shan of his own guilt. Now, at last, Shan
knew the truth.

Jay Bennett

"You killed him. Liar!" Lambert struck him again, this time a slashing blow with the barrel of the gun. Shan sank to his knees, his head reeling with pain, yet he still cried out.

"You're the liar. You knew he did it. You knew. But you couldn't face the truth. Then it would have been your fault!"

"Stop it! Stop it!" Lambert raised the gun to strike at Shan again, but this time, with a last effort of desperation, Shan lunged forward and caught him hard just below the knees and toppled him over. Lambert fell hard to the floor, with Shan on him. Shan hit him with all his remaining strength, again and again, until he heard a gasp, and then he stopped.

Shan slowly got to his feet. He stood, swaying, and then he groped around till he found the gun. It was only after he had found it that he thought of putting on the light. Then he staggered over to the bed and sat down on it.

He held the gun tightly in his fist, pointed at the fallen man.

XXVII

They sat together on a bench, gazing out over the park lake. The two had talked quietly, and now there was a pause.

"Shan."

"Yes, Donna?"

"In a way I feel so sorry for him. Even after all he did to you."

Shan's hand went to the strip of bandage on his cheek and jaw. He didn't say anything.

"You still hate him?"

He shook his head. "No, Donna," he finally said. "I . . . I just hope they can do things for him. Give him the treatment that he needs. And that it works for him. Maybe he's too far gone. I don't know."

He got up and stood there looking at the reflection of the sun, pale and shimmering on the water. Then he stooped and with his left hand picked up a flat stone and scaled it over the water. He watched it skip along and then sink. His right hand hung at his side, still swollen from the burns.

He sighed. "My mother is still pretty broken up about it all."

"She loved him, Shan."

He scaled another stone and didn't comment.

"And even after everything, she . . . she . . ." Donna didn't finish.

"She still loves him," he said in an even voice.

"You feel bitter about that, don't you?"

He turned away from the lake and faced her. "Yes," he said. He came over and sat next to her on the bench.

"When do you see Dr. Loeb again?"

"Tomorrow. He's been helping me a lot. I look forward to my sessions with him." He turned to her and smiled. "We're trying to figure out whether what I said to Lambert was true or not."

"You mean whether George killed himself? Or you . . . ?"

"Uh-huh."

"And what do you think, Shan?"

"I think George committed suicide, but it doesn't really matter to me anymore," he said gently. "I've lost my sense of guilt over it all. Whatever happened, I was a child then. And now I'm beginning to think maybe I'm growing to be a man."

"Maybe you are, Shan," she said softly.

She put her arms about him, and they kissed.